Red stain
12/7/08 ST

What Teens Are Saying About
DIARY OF A TEENAGE GIRL SERIES...

"I couldn't put this book down! Reading *I Do!* made me much closer to God. Melody Carlson is a great author. I've read all of her Chloe books in less than a month."—BRITTANY

"I really enjoyed *It's My Life.* As a teenager, it's hard to find that book that really touches your soul about issues teen girls face each day. Melody Carlson does a wonderful job of ministering to me and to show me that God will always be there for me. I can't think of anything better than that."—DANA

"*My Name Is Chloe* is really AMAZING! I like the characters and the way the story is written. I read this book in two days, it was so good. I can't wait to get the next one."—PORSCHE

"I was really needing something inspirational in my life, and *Face the Music* came at the right time! Melody is a great writer!"—JAIME

"I loved *My Name Is Chloe* so much. I can relate to Chloe in so many ways. I am fifteen years old. I have been a Christian all my life, but I went though a rebellious stage. Luckily I'm back on track."—TAYLOR

"I absolutely love this whole series! I'm on the last book of the Caitlin series, and then I hope to start the Chloe series. These books got me closer to God, and I'm so glad that I've read them."—CIERRA

"*Becoming Me* inspired me! I am now closer to God myself and understand life more in a positive way. I look forward to reading the rest of the series and growing closer to God as Caitlin does. I highly recommend this book."—KAETLYN

Diary of a Teenage Girl

Kim Book N⁰. 1

Just Ask

a novel

MELODY CARLSON

Multnomah® Publishers
Sisters, Oregon

JUST ASK
published by Multnomah Publishers, Inc.
and in association with the literary agency of Sara A. Fortenberry

© 2005 by Carlson Management Co., Inc.
International Standard Book Number: 1-59052-321-0

Cover design by studiogearbox.com
Cover image by Gen Nishino/Getty Images

For information:
MULTNOMAH PUBLISHERS, INC.
601 N. LARCH ST.
SISTERS, OREGON 97759

05 06 07 08 09 10—10 9 8 7 6 5 4 3 2 1 0

Books by Melody Carlson:

Piercing Proverbs

DIARY OF A TEENAGE GIRL SERIES
<u>Caitlin O'Conner</u>:
Becoming Me
It's My Life
Who I Am
On My Own
I Do!
<u>Chloe Miller</u>:
My Name Is Chloe
Sold Out
Road Trip
Face the Music
<u>Kim Peterson</u>:
Just Ask
Meant to Be (October 2005)

TRUE COLOR SERIES
Dark Blue, color me lonely
Deep Green, color me jealous
Torch Red, color me torn
Pitch Black, color me lost
Burnt Orange, color me wasted
Fool's Gold, color me consumed

One

Thursday, September 1

I never would've guessed that my own father would resort to using blackmail against me. I mean, I'm his only daughter, his "little princess" even. But it seems my dad has sunk to a new low lately. I suppose it's just the desperate cry of a frustrated newspaperman who lives in a rather small and boring town where big news only happens once in a great while. Like the time that guy went bonkers and shot a bunch of kids at McFadden High.

I was still in middle school then, but the whole town was turned inside out over the senseless tragedy. All the big news networks flew in, and my dad ran stories in his paper for weeks—some that were even picked up by United Press International. He actually keeps those articles framed and hanging above his desk, which I personally think is kind of flaky, but I don't let on.

It's not like we want these particular sorts of disasters (like the McFadden shooting) to happen on a regular basis exactly, but as my dad says, "That's what sells papers."

Of course, we have other kinds of news too. Our local paper recently enjoyed the celebrity of the Christian rock band Redemption. Which is one of the reasons my dad started a new section in the paper called Teen Beat. A pretty lame name if you ask me, although he didn't. Anyway, I do go the extra mile to keep him informed of Redemption's latest news (like when they won a music award last spring). And that seems to keep him happy. Well, most of the time.

The reason I keep him up-to-date on Redemption is because Chloe Miller (leader of the band) is a pretty good friend. I've actually known her for years, not just after she became rich and famous. There are those user-types who really take advantage of her generous nature. Like "Chloe is my best friend" just because they had one conversation with her. But here's what's weird—she actually lets them use her like that.

She says it's because she's a Christian. Yeah, right. I mean, just because you're a Christian doesn't mean you should let people walk all over you, does it? Not that she really lets people walk on her like that. But it's like she doesn't really mind either. And this seriously confuses me.

Still, I do like and respect Chloe, and despite her whole Christianity thing, she seems like a genuinely real person to me. And even though she knows that I'm not so sure about the whole religion thing myself, she treats me like I'm a decent human being and worthy of respect.

And I can't say that about all Christians. I mean, we have some kids at our school who are always trying to evangelize EVERYONE. And if you're not interested in listening to them, they snub you and treat you like you're Satan or just plain hopeless.

It's not like I'm a "perfect heathen," as my mom sometimes teases when I skip out on church—something I've been doing a lot lately. But it's not like I don't know what goes on there. I mean, I used to go pretty regularly with my parents (well, only because they made me), and okay, I'm sure it's just fine for <u>some</u> people, but it's not for me.

And it's not because my parents go to an "old-fashioned" church (as my best friend likes to call it). In fact, I actually kind of like the oldness to it—the reverent sounds of the organ playing up in the loft, the rich hues of stained glass, and the pungent smell of wood oil on the pews. But that's about where it stops for me. The rest of it is like one giant snooze. And frankly I'd rather do that in the comfort of my own bed.

Fortunately, I was able to avoid church most of the time this past summer thanks to my job at the mall, which I had to give up because school was starting and my parents felt a job would be "too distracting" to my education. Yeah, sure!

Anyway, back to my dad and how he's blackmailing his only daughter. I got my driver's license last year, and I've been saving for my own car ever since. My parents told me that they'd match what I've saved when I'm ready to get one. And I was almost ready.

But then my parents cooked up this little deal. Mostly it's my mom's idea, since she saw this show on "Oprah," and now she's totally freaked that I'm going to drive recklessly and get myself killed. They decided that I could only get a car if I keep a clean driving record. That means absolutely NO tickets—period—nada.

So as usual, I was driving my mom's car to work yesterday. And her car's just this frumpy 1998 Buick LeSabre (not exactly a race car if you know what I mean). It was my last day to go to work, I'd forgotten to set my alarm, and I was running a little late. So you can imagine my surprise when I heard that wailing siren and saw those flashing red and blue lights in my rearview mirror.

Now, if I'd been a praying kind of person, I would've begged God to spare me from getting a speeding ticket, but I am not. The policeman said he'd clocked me going seventy-two in a fifty-five-mile zone. Oops.

"You were going seventeen miles over the speed limit, young lady." He relayed this information to me as if he thought I was unable to do simple math. I almost considered telling him that I was the mental math champion throughout grade school but felt pretty sure it wouldn't help my case. I'm not stupid; in fact that's exactly why I gave up showing off my academic superiority several years ago. It never seems to help anything.

"But <u>everyone</u> drives sixty-five through here," I told him in what I hoped was a respectful tone. "So it's more like I was only going <u>seven</u> miles over the limit." I guess I actually hoped he'd change the ticket or something.

But this man had no mercy for speeding teenage girls. "The law's the law." He had a serious expression as he handed me the ticket. "You better slow down before you get hurt."

I actually cried when I looked down at the ticket. Not just because it was for $285, but also because I knew this would mean <u>no car</u>.

After work, I went straight to my dad's newspaper.

"Daddy," I began in my sweetest <u>little princess</u> voice. "I have something to tell you, and I don't want you to get mad. Okay?"

I could tell by his expression that he was expecting the worst. Like what would that be? Did he think I was pregnant or had a bad coke-snorting habit or was wanted by the FBI or what? Anyway, I slowly told him my sad story, making it as pitiful as possible. But I could sense his relief that it wasn't something way more serious.

"I'm really sorry, Daddy. And I promise I won't speed again. I'm sure I've learned my lesson, and I plan to pay the whole fine myself."

I managed to actually work up a few tears (I'm in

drama and love putting on a good show). "I just don't know what I'll do if I can't get my own car now. I cannot ride that hideous school bus, Daddy. Think how stupid I will look. And I can't have Mom dropping me off. How lame is that? I mean, I'm a <u>junior</u> this year. Only a geek would ride the school bus or have her mom drop her off."

I waited for a moment. Then when he looked unconvinced, I told him some horror stories about what happens to geeky kids who ride the bus.

"Oh, Kim," he said. "I think you're exaggerating."

So I put on my best pouty face and pulled out my trump card. See, what I haven't told you yet is, although my parents are of the all-American white-bread Caucasian variety, I myself happen to be Asian. Korean in fact. I was adopted as an infant, and occasionally I can really make it work for me.

"And sometimes I get teased for being, well, you know, different," I told my dad with some dramatic hesitation. Now this isn't completely untrue. But I have to admit, I was really working it just then.

"Oh, honey." My dad sighed and shook his head, and I wasn't sure if he felt bad or was seeing right through me. After all, as a managing editor of a newspaper, he is pretty good at sniffing out the truth.

"<u>Really</u>, Daddy. The kids on the bus can be so mean. Sometimes they even call me names." And then I actually repeat a couple of slang words that my dad <u>cannot</u> stand to hear. Words that have actually been used against me in the past; unkind words I try to forget.

And that's when I knew I almost had him where I wanted him.

He got this thoughtful expression as he drummed his pencil up and down like a skinny woodpecker pecking on the rim of his coffee cup. Then he pressed his lips tightly together in that I-am-getting-an-idea sort of look. And that started to scare me.

"Okay, Kim, how about this?" He paused to study me for what felt like a full minute before he continued. "How about if we keep this one ticket between you and me?"

"Really?" I could hardly believe my good fortune. This was way easier than I'd expected.

He nodded. "But only if you agree to do something in return."

"Huh?"

"I want you to write the advice column for Teen Beat."

"Oh, Daddy!" I frowned as I sunk into the chair across from his desk. My dad had been pestering me all summer to do this stupid column for him. He honestly thought that teens would write letters to his newspaper—just like "Dear Abby"—and that they would actually read the answers some lame person (hopefully, not me!) wrote back in response.

"Come on, Kim, we're making a deal here. Are you in or not?"

"Daddy." I slouched lower into the chair and folded my arms across my chest; I tried my pouting routine again.

But he wasn't falling for it this time. "You're a talented writer, sweetheart. And you've got a good head on your shoulders. Plus you're very mature for your age. Honestly, I really think you can do this."

"But I don't <u>want</u> to do this." I sat up straight and looked him right in the eyes now. "Don't you understand how stupid I would look? I don't want kids going around school saying 'Kim Peterson writes that lame advice column in Teen Beat. Like who does she think she is anyway?'"

He held up his hands to stop me. "No, no, you don't understand, Kim. You have to remain anonymous for it to work. We'll give you a pseudonym or something. No one must know who writes the column."

"Really?"

"Of course."

"And you really wouldn't tell Mom about my speeding ticket?"

"It'll be part of our deal. You don't tell anyone you're writing this column for me, and I won't tell Mom that you got the ticket."

"And I can still get a car?"

He nodded. "And you'll even get paid for writing."

"I'll get paid?"

He shrugged. "Well, not much, honey. But we'll work out something."

And so that's how I got stuck with this small pile of letters (supposedly from teens) for "Just Ask Jamie"— that's the actual name of the advice column. Of course,

Dad didn't just ask if I wanted it called that. But I guess it's okay. Although I wish he'd come up with something better for my pseudonym than Jamie. But he wanted to use a unisex name so kids wouldn't know whether I was a guy or girl. Well, whatever.

Also, my dad has linked me up with some "resources" for any tricky questions that might involve the law or anything outside of my expertise. "Like what exactly is my expertise?" I asked him. He just laughed and assured me that I would be fine. We'll see.

Anyway, I've just finished practicing my violin (I have to get back into shape before school starts), and I decided I would "practice write" my answers to these letters in the safety zone of my own computer diary (which is accessible only with my secret password). I figure this will help me see whether I can really pull this thing off or not. I've picked the first letter to answer. Mostly I picked this one because it's a pretty basic question, no biggie. So here goes nothing.

Dear Jamie,

I am fifteen years old, and I desperately want to get my belly button pierced. My mom says, "Not as long as you're living under my roof!" But I say, "Hey, it's my belly button, and it should be up to me if I want to put a hole in it or not." Right? Anyway, I plan to get it done soon. And I've decided not to tell my mom. Do you think I'm wrong to secretly do this?

Holeyer than Some

Dear Holeyer,

   While I can totally understand wanting to pierce your belly button—because I, too, happen to think that looks pretty cool when done right—I really think you should consider some things first. Like how is your mom going to feel when she finds out you did this behind her back? Because moms always find out. And how will this mess up your relationship with her? Because whether you like it or not, you'll probably be stuck living "under her roof" for about three more years. So why not try to talk this thing through with her? Explain that you could go behind her back, but you'd rather have her permission. Believe me, you'll enjoy your pierced belly button a whole lot more if you don't pierce your mom's heart along with it.

   Just Jamie

Okay, now I have a problem. I feel like a total hypocrite because I haven't been completely honest with <u>my</u> mom. Oh, sure, I didn't go out and pierce my belly button. Although that might not be as bad as breaking the law, getting a ticket, and then not telling her. Of course, my dad <u>did</u> make a deal with me when he blackmailed me with the advice column. So maybe this is different. But if this is different, why do I feel guilty? Maybe I should write a letter to Jamie and <u>just ask</u>!

TWO

Friday, September 2

My dad actually liked the responses I wrote for the "Just Ask Jamie" column. I'm not sure whether to be hugely relieved or totally freaked. Like who am I to be giving advice to kids my own age? What do I really know about life anyway? Still, my dad seems to have confidence in me. And besides, even if I totally blow at this, at least no one will ever know who this Jamie weirdo really is. That's some consolation.

Mostly I keep reminding myself that writing this column means I might soon have my own wheels. Even so, I felt pretty nervous when I saw my column appear in bold black and white in today's newspaper (the plan is to run it biweekly, on Tuesdays and Fridays).

To distract myself from obsessing over this column or, more specifically, how kids will react to my so-called "advice" (assuming they'll even read it, which is seriously doubtful), I've been focusing my attention on this bright yellow Jeep Wrangler parked across the street. I've always thought it was pretty cool looking, but our neighbor just put a For Sale on it yesterday.

As soon as I saw that sign go up, I could barely stand it. I mean, what if someone else sees this great little Jeep and buys it before I have a chance? Because it's not only totally awesome, but it's also totally perfect for me. At least that's my opinion. And after going on and on about it last night, my dad finally agreed that we could take it for a test drive tomorrow morning. He even made an appointment with Carl. And I cannot wait.

Mom's all worried about safety issues now. She thinks that just because it has a soft top, I'll probably roll it the first time out and kill myself. I tried to explain to her the purpose of a "roll bar," but that didn't seem to help matters. Finally I asked Carl, the Jeep owner, to convince my mom that it's perfectly fine. He promised to do his best.

I'm also going online to collect all the best safety data I can find on Jeeps. Of course, I'll be very discerning in what I allow my mom to read. Probably I'll just stick to the manufacturer's claims and promises. That should assure her I'll be safe behind the wheel of my new fun mobile. Oh, I can see myself now.

"Are you really getting that Jeep?" my best friend Natalie McCabe asked me after we jogged this morning. (We've been trying to get into better shape before school starts—her idea, of course, and I suspect a few days of exercise is not enough to make much difference.)

Nat lives two houses down from me, and we've been best friends since fourth grade. Okay, on and off best friends. Sometimes she really aggravates me, and I suppose I've made her mad more than once too. But most of the time I don't know what I'd do without her. I guess she's the closet thing to a sister I'll ever have.

I paused to run my hand over the smooth surface of the hood. Carl had just waxed and detailed everything, and even though it was four years old, it looked like it could've been on a showroom floor. "I hope so," I told her. "Dad and I are going to try it out tomorrow."

"You are so lucky," she said in what sounded like a slightly jealous voice.

"Hey, you'll get to ride in it too."

She brightened then. "Oh, yeah. That's true. Okay, then I hope you get it, Kim. I'll be praying really hard that your parents will agree."

Now this is one area where Natalie and I seriously part ways. I mean, she is so into this whole church, God, and praying thing, but I try not to let this get to me. And after this one ripsnorting disagreement last spring, I think she learned that it's wise to watch what she says around me.

"Thanks," I told her. "Maybe I'll get it in time to drive us to school the first day."

"That'd sure beat driving my old Toyota," she said. Natalie's dad left this cruddy old pickup behind when he walked out on his wife and three kids last year.

"Which reminds me," she said. "Do you want to go to the mall with me today? I just got paid, and I still need to get a couple of things for school."

"I guess." I reluctantly turned away from my dream Jeep. "But I don't see why you bother to get new clothes for school, Nat. What difference does it make if you wear something old or something new?"

She laughed as she glanced down at my old sweats. "I just keep hoping you're going to figure that one out, Kim."

As usual I rolled my eyes at her, hopefully avoiding another you-have-absolutely-no-fashion-sense lecture. Yeah, whatever.

So it was settled that we'd go around two. In the meantime, I needed to practice my violin and then answer some more of these crazy letters. My dad just e-mailed me a whole new bunch today. But as I read through them, I'm beginning to wonder if these are really for real.

I mean, some of them are just totally bizarre. Like this one letter from a girl who's all bent out of shape because her little brother dressed up her male Chihuahua like a ballerina. And now she's worried that her dog might have a complex. Give me a break! Like a dog dressed in drag is going to need canine counseling or something.

Well, I don't think I'll even answer that one. That is, unless Tuesday's column needs a little comic relief. And considering some of the other heavier topics, it just might. Like this one letter I saved for last, since I had to call one of my resources for some additional input.

Dear Jamie,

My parents split up a few years ago. My dad moved away with his new girlfriend who's like only twenty, and I haven't heard from him since. My mom works at a minimum-wage job and couldn't even pay rent and stuff if I didn't help her from my job, which actually pays better than hers. And I didn't really mind helping either, but now she has this new jerk of a boyfriend who moved in with us. He doesn't even have a job and is a total loser. Not only does he eat all our food and make big messes, but he's been putting the move on me lately. I'm only sixteen, but I think I could make it on my own, and I've heard that kids can divorce their parents. What do you think? Should I divorce my mom?

Fed Up

Dear Fed Up,

Wow, I can see why you're frustrated. First of all, I think you should talk to your mom and tell her what you're considering. But if she refuses to kick the loser boyfriend out, you should probably check out some other alternatives. According to my resources, you may not need to go as far as divorcing your mom (and it sounds kind of expensive). But you should make an appointment with a Family Services counselor and

*explain what's going on. And if you have another
relative or acceptable place to live, they can probably
work it out so you can move out without going into
foster care. But hopefully your mom will figure things
out, and you'll be able to remain at home. If not, I hope
that you don't cut yourself off from her completely. I'm
guessing that her loser boyfriend won't be around for
long, but she'll always be your mother.*

    Just Jamie

Now I'm thinking about my own mom and how
she'd do just about anything for me. Really, if I needed a
heart transplant, I'll bet she'd offer me her own. Not that
I'd let her, of course. But she's just like that.

My parents got married way back in the seventies,
and my mom's dream had always been to have kids,
but she had some health problems that made it
impossible to get pregnant. After years and years of
trying everything, my parents looked into adoption, but
the waiting lists for American babies was so long, they
decided to look outside of the country. Naturally, this is
where I came in.

My parents finally discovered this international
adoption service that happened to be linked to the
Korean orphanage where I'd been "dropped off." And by
the time I was six months old, I was shipped off (well,
flown, actually) to the United States where I became a
part of the Peterson family of three.

I asked my parents why they didn't send off for more

Korean babies (since Mom had always wanted a houseful of kids), but they said they both agreed that I was more than enough.

I've never been quite sure how to take that, since I've heard through friends and relatives that I was a very fussy baby. But I do know that they love me and probably wouldn't trade me for a backseat full of quiet and well-behaved orphans.

But when I think about this girl (Fed Up) and how her parents seem like they could care less about her, well, I guess it's times like this when I really question life in general. I mean, why do some people long for children but are unable to have them? And then other people can have children, but they desert them as infants? And why do some parents have kids of their own and then abandon them when they become teens? Does any of this make any sense?

I think it's things like this that made me start questioning God and religion in the first place. I mean, if life doesn't make sense, how can God make sense?

Well, it was questions like this that motivated me last spring to learn more about the religion of my ancestors. To be fair, it probably began about the same time Chloe Miller challenged me about what I believe.

"I was brought up as a Christian," I tell her during one of our first conversations about religion. "But I'm just not into it anymore."

"Why not?" she asks.

"I guess I don't buy it."

"I didn't know it was for sale," she shoots back at me. And I am thinking, yeah, very funny.

"Well, I suppose it was okay when I was a little girl. But now it just seems like some worn-out old fairy tale. I mean, think about all those totally whacked-out stories in the Bible, like the Noah dude building a boat and filling it with every species of animals on the planet and—"

"Hey, I was just reading about how scientists have discovered archaeological evidence which proves that really happened," she tells me.

And so we went, back and forth, but not in an argumentative way. She never made me feel bad about my questioning things. If anything, she totally validated me. "I used to do the exact same thing," she tells me. "I questioned absolutely everything about God. But then He revealed Himself to me."

"And you _quit_ questioning?" I remember how skeptical I felt at what sounded like a pat answer to me. It reminded me of something our pastor might say.

"Not at all," she assures me. "I still question tons of things. Only now I take my questions directly to God."

"And I suppose He answers you?"

She kind of smiles then. "Well, not in words exactly. Sometimes it's through the Bible or people or just life in general. But the answers usually come eventually. Oh, not for everything, of course. I guess there are some things we just have to wait on."

But she got me thinking. And I had to admit that there seemed to be something missing in my life. Kind of like a hole or a gap or a vacuum. I couldn't even really describe it. But maybe it was religion.

But that didn't mean it had to be the Christian religion. To be honest, I felt like I'd had my fill of that. So I decided to check out my own Korean roots. And after I looked into Chundoism (which turned out to be a more modern Korean religion that actually had some roots in Christianity), I decided to go a little further back in time. And that's when I began to investigate Buddhism.

I got some books from the library and then went online to research everything I could find. And believe me, there's a lot. And a lot of it is pretty confusing too. At least at first. But if you sort of relax your brain a little and just think about it awhile, it starts to sink in. Then if you boil it down to the basics, it slowly begins to make a little sense. And in some ways, it's not all that different from Christianity.

Take the Five Precepts (kind of like the Ten Commandments). Basically they are: 1) Don't kill, but be kind. 2) Don't steal, but be generous. 3) Control your lust, and practice awareness. 4) Don't lie or gossip, but use good words. 5) Don't use intoxicants, but think clearly.

Now really, is there anything wrong with any of that? I didn't think so. But when my parents (mostly my mom) heard me talking about my exploration into Buddhism, well, you'd think that I'd told them I wanted to worship the devil.

After my mom stopped crying, my dad told her that

it probably wasn't such a bad thing. "Knowledge is good," he said. "And Kim is an intelligent girl. She'll discover the truth in time."

I wasn't exactly sure what he meant by this "discover the truth in time" line. Like did he think that I'd get tired of Buddhism and go back to their Christian ways of thinking? But his words seemed to appease my mom, and at the time, that was good enough for me.

Consequently, I've been much more discreet about my Buddhism research. And for the sake of family and friends, I try to keep quiet about my religious journey. Chloe is the only one I ever talk to about stuff like this. And thankfully, she doesn't ever put me down.

And some things about Buddhism I really like. For one thing, Buddhists don't criticize other religions. They sort of believe that all religions eventually lead to truth. And that's kind of cool. Buddhism has a lot to do with the mind and practicing self-control and gaining understanding. Nothing wrong with that.

But I do have one little problem with Buddhism. Okay, maybe it's a big problem. But it has to do with karma, which I used to think was pretty cool, until I discovered more about it.

I began studying the Four Noble Truths (foundational in Buddhism), and I got a little confused by the belief that everything that happens to you (good or bad) is essentially your own fault. Now, it's not like I don't want to take the blame for something when it's really my fault (like, say, when I got that speeding ticket and got stuck writing the column), but what about things that I have absolutely no control over?

For instance, I was abandoned at birth. According to the Second Noble Truth, this must be my fault. So maybe I cried too much as a baby. Or maybe my diapers were really nasty and stinky. I don't know. But I don't see how you can blame a baby for the fact that its parents don't want it anymore. That just seems wrong.

And today as I wrote back to Fed Up, I didn't see how it could possibly be <u>her</u> fault that her parents split up and started acting like total morons. It's messing up her life and causing her grief, and I just don't get that.

So I am a little confused about Buddhism too and have decided not to think about religion any more today. Instead I plan to think about test-driving that cool Jeep Wrangler tomorrow. And in the meantime, I will take the time to answer one more letter. Hopefully, nothing as serious as Fed Up's letter.

Dear Jamie,

I'm thirteen and totally freaking about something I did. It happened at summer camp. You see, my friend "Amy" and I wanted to do something outrageous and shocking to get attention. So we pulled off a fake-bi (where we actually kissed each other just like Madonna and Britney). Naturally, we did this while all our friends were looking, and at the time it seemed pretty hilarious.

But now I am seriously worried that when we go back to school next week, everyone will be saying we're lesbians. What should I do?

Freaked Faker

P.S. Do you think we might actually be lesbians but don't really know it yet?

Dear Freaked,

I seriously doubt you and your friend are lesbians. But I do think your fake-bi was pretty lame. You guys need to remember how easy it is to send the wrong message—and how hard it is to take it back. So you and "Amy" will probably have to straighten people out with the news that you're straight too. Next time, you might want to look before you leap.

Just Jamie

Three

Saturday, September 3

All right! Dad and I test-drove the Jeep today, and I immediately got the sense that he thought it was a great little vehicle. I mean, he started talking about taking it out in the woods and camping and stuff. So I promised him that he could drive it occasionally if he'd just let me get it. Of course, I doubt my offer had that much influence, but he did talk to my mom, and after about an hour of discussion (while I was scrubbing down the entire kitchen), she finally caved.

So this afternoon, I gave Carl my down payment, signed a sales agreement with my dad (since he's carrying my loan), and I am now the proud owner of a Jeep Wrangler. Woo-hoo!

The first thing I do (after taking my mom for a nice little ride to reassure her that the Jeep is perfectly safe) is to call Natalie and invite her to go cruising with me.

"This is so awesome, Kim!" she shrieks as she jumps in and figures out how to close the door. I've already taken the soft top off so we can drive to town in style. And it turns out that Carl also had a "hard" top for wintertime use. This really helped to bring my mom on board.

"Thanks," I tell Natalie as I look both ways before I pull out onto the street. Believe me, I am being very careful about driving now. No way do I want to mess this baby up.

"You are so lucky!" she says as she tries out the CD player. I already loaded it with my favorite CDs.

"I know!" And I can tell that I've got this goofy-looking smile plastered all over my face as I drive toward town with the wind blowing through my hair. But honestly, I am so happy I can barely contain myself. This is so cool.

"I mean, seriously, Kim. I thought you'd never get a car after that major speeding ticket you racked up last week. I just cannot believe your parents gave in like that."

I'd almost forgotten that Natalie knew about my stupid ticket. "Hey, don't forget that I swore you to secrecy."

"But what's the difference now that you've got your own wheels?"

"Well, it's because of this deal that my dad and I worked out," I admit without filling in the details. "My mom doesn't know about it. I don't want you to say anything."

She kind of frowns now. "You mean you're lying to your mom?"

"Not exactly. It's just that my dad wanted to work this thing out in his own way. He didn't want to upset my mom. You know how she gets so freaked about the smallest things."

Natalie nods. "I can still remember when you broke your arm in fifth grade. I thought your mom was going to have a heart attack right there at the swimming pool."

"Yeah, that's exactly what I'm talking about."

"But you're so lucky that your dad's cool with this kind of stuff," she says as I turn to cruise down Main Street. Okay, I know it's kinda lame, but I just can't help myself. I really hope we see someone we know.

"Dad's made it totally clear that if I get another ticket of any kind, I won't be driving anything besides my bike." I slow way down as soon as I see the business zone sign. I'm not taking any chances.

We decide to stop in at the Paradiso Café for coffee. But I park right in front so I can keep an eye on my Jeep. "I wonder if this is how a new mom feels," I say to Natalie as we get out, and I pocket my new set of keys. "Like I don't want to leave my Jeep out of sight for even a minute."

She looks at me like I might be losing it. "I seriously doubt that a mom would leave her baby out on the street, Kim." Then I give her my do-you-know-what-you-just-said look, and suddenly her blue eyes grow wide. "Oh, I'm sorry, Kim," she says quickly. "I forgot about what happened in Korea—"

"It's okay," I tell her. Then I pat the Jeep's hood. "I'd take you inside the coffeehouse, Daisy, but I don't think you'd fit through the door."

"You named your Jeep?"

"Of course." I grin. I do sound pretty ridiculous. "It's not like you have to tell anyone about it. But honestly, doesn't she look like a Daisy to you?"

Natalie just laughs as if she thinks my sanity might be questionable. But I don't really care. Let her laugh. I'm the one who got the keys to a totally great set of wheels today.

"Hey, there," calls a somewhat familiar voice as soon as we walk into the Paradiso. I glance over to my right and see Cesar Rodriguez and Jake Hall sitting by the window.

"Hey," I call back. "How are you guys doing?"

"Not bad." Cesar smiles that killer smile of his, and I have to wonder why someone from Hollywood hasn't discovered this gorgeous Latino yet. And as usual, that makes me wonder, how was it that Chloe ever gave him up? Or did he give her up? I still don't know for sure. I guess it's none of my business either.

"You girls want to join us?" asks Jake.

I glance at Natalie, and she just shrugs like that's okay.

"Sure," I tell them. "We'll go order first."

Now Natalie and I don't really fit into any specific group at school. Not so you'd notice anyway. I suppose if anything you'd call us academics—we are in Honor

Society—although I like to imagine that we're not as geeky as some of our academic peers.

Though I did get a serious scare in freshman English a couple of years back. Mrs. Samuels pointed me out as the "girl with the perfect grammar." Eeeuuu! I mean, who wants to be <u>that</u>? So I went out of my way to start talking just like everyone else. It's like I became sort of a pop-culture linguist of sorts. Naturally, my parents totally hate it. But sometimes a girl has to do what a girl has to do to fit in. Not that I <u>fit in</u> so well. But at least I don't stick out quite so much now.

And while Natalie and I aren't exactly the popular smiley-faced cheerleader types (which is actually fine with me since I tend to think those girls are pretty shallow and superficial anyway), we're not total losers either. But we don't go out for sports, so we're not jocks. And we're not into things like chess club or debate team, so we're not really nerds (at least we don't think so). But we do participate in drama sometimes. Although we're not totally devoted to every single production either—so we're not really drama freaks either. Maybe we're not really anything.

Actually, I think we see ourselves more as observers, or fringers, like sometimes we might even feel slightly invisible. As a result, we don't have a whole mob of friends either. Like huge understatement. But that may have as much to do with being picky as it does with not being picked.

Oh, it's not that people dislike us, but more that they simply don't really notice us. And trust me, sometimes

<u>not</u> being noticed is a whole lot better than being
noticed, if you know what I mean. 'Cause everyone
who's been in middle school knows that kids can be
really cruel. Especially girls.

"Kim?" Natalie says, like she's already said it more
than once. "It's your turn to order now."

I order a cappuccino, which is the coolest coffee
drink, then quietly ask Natalie if she's okay sitting with
those guys.

"It's cool." She pretends to toss some of her long
blond hair over one shoulder, but I can tell she's just
using this as an excuse to look back at their table. Then
she smiles. "But I get to sit by Cesar."

I laugh at this. "Yeah, whatever." I don't bother to
mention that Cesar doesn't date. I only know this
because of Chloe. The fact is, I've only gotten to know
Cesar through Chloe, and I don't really know him all that
well. But he and Jake have been friends with Chloe for a
couple of years now.

Last spring, during a time when Nat and I weren't
speaking (thankfully it lasted only a week or two), Chloe
kind of befriended me and pulled me into their group a
few times. I even got to jam with the band once. Pretty
cool.

But I actually like these two guys, and in some ways
they remind me of Natalie and me. Like none of us are
quite sure where we fit in exactly. But maybe that's okay.
And maybe they're the kind of guys who Nat and I can
fit in with.

We get our coffees and go back to join them.
Naturally, I let Natalie sit next to Cesar as promised. And
I sit next to Jake (who always reminds me of that
comedian Carrot Top—only Jake's not such a maniac).

"You guys ready for school to start?" I ask as I blow a
little hole in the milky foam that tops my cappuccino.

Jake groans. "No way."

Cesar shrugs. "Yeah, sort of."

"Did you see Kim's new set of wheels?" Natalie nods
toward the window where my Jeep is clearly visible.

Jake looks out with interest. "Which one?"

"That yellow Jeep," I tell them, watching for their
reactions.

"Cool," says Cesar with an approving nod.

"Way cool," agrees Jake.

I smile. Owning a good car is one way to get some
guys' attention.

"Yeah," says Natalie. "Kim's an only child, and her
parents spoil her rotten…their little Asian princess." Then
she winks at me because she knows this always makes
me want to scream and pull my hair out.

"Oh, sure, that's why I worked my tail off all summer
just to have a down payment, because I'm so spoiled."

"But how will you keep paying for it?" she asks,
"now that you're not working anymore?"

I consider this. No way am I going to mention my
newspaper column job. "Don't worry; my parents think
I'm their personal slave." Then I give them this sly look
and lower my voice. "Don't you know that's why all

these American parents send away to get kids from other countries? It's just this big cover-up for child slavery. John Stossel from '20/20' just called to see if he can do an exposé that features my parents and me."

"Yeah, you bet." Natalie rolls her big blue eyes at me. "If anyone does an exposé on child slavery, they better shoot it at my house. Honestly, my mom was in such a hormonal snit this morning, I couldn't even leave until I'd totally vacuumed and dusted every square inch of our whole freaking house. And Krissy and Micah do nothing but create more messes."

Krissy and Micah are her younger siblings (only eight and ten years old and not very helpful). But despite Natalie's complaints, I know she loves them both a lot. But I also know that Mrs. McCabe has gone through a lot of pretty weird mood swings since Natalie's dad ran out on them last year. Not that you can blame her exactly. I mean, he gave them absolutely no warning, just hooked up with a coworker and took off.

And I know it hasn't been easy for Natalie either, since she picks up a lot of the slack with Krissy and Micah, but usually she manages to maintain a fairly brave front. I figure she must be feeling pretty bummed today.

"Okay," I tell her. "You win. I'll send John and his crew over to your house for the exposé."

She kind of smiles now. "Thanks. Sorry to dump like that."

This is one of those times when I try to give her

some space. And I try not to get too aggravated if she acts like my life is so perfect. Mostly I know she doesn't really mean it; she's just hurting over her family's troubles. And hey, maybe she is a little jealous.

We talk and joke some more, and Natalie's mood slowly improves. Then the table gets quiet, and Jake picks up the newspaper that's sitting at his elbow. "Did you guys see this new teen column?"

I take in a quick breath. Just chill. Remain calm. Do not give anything away. "No, what is it?"

"Don't you even read your dad's newspaper?" Natalie knows this embarrasses me.

"Your dad owns the paper?" asks Cesar.

I laugh. "No, he just acts like it. Actually, he's the managing editor."

"Well, you should read this advice column." Jake turns to the Teen Beat page and hands it to me.

Now I can't tell, by the tone of his voice, whether he approves of it or not. But I am getting seriously unnerved as I take the newspaper and pretend to skim over the very words I wrote earlier this week. "Yeah, so?"

"Don't you think it's funny?" he asks.

"What do you mean?"

"You must not have read the one about the girl who caught her uncle trying on her grandma's nightgown," says Natalie, suppressing laughter. "Jamie's response was hilarious. She has such a great sense of humor."

"How do you know it's a she?" asks Cesar. "I think Jamie must be a guy."

"No way," argues Natalie. "Jamie's got to be a girl."

And on they go arguing over Jamie's gender. In order to continue my charade, I take turns on different sides as I attempt to act unimpressed by the column in general. But it seems fairly clear that Cesar and Natalie actually like it. Jake's still not quite sure.

"I don't know..." he says. "I think I would've told the belly-button girl to just go ahead and pierce it. I mean, it's her body. Why should her parents get to decide what she does with her own belly button anyway?"

"Of course you'd think that." Natalie points to the dragon climbing up his arm. "I mean, you've got a tattoo. Did your parents give you permission to do that?"

He laughs. "Hey, they were so checked out at the time. Like they never even noticed it for about a year or so."

"And what did they do then?" I ask.

He shrugs. "Nothing." But his eyes seem sort of sad, and I suspect that he'd hoped for a bigger reaction.

"Hey, have you heard from Chloe lately?" I ask Cesar, thinking we must be about ready for a new subject by now.

"Not for a couple of weeks. But I think their concert tour is really tough this time. It's taking a lot out of them. It sounds like they play almost every other night."

"Won't they be home soon?" I ask.

"Yeah. They're supposed to be back in school this fall."

"That's cool," I say. "I felt like I was just getting to know Chloe again last spring."

"She's great," says Cesar.

Jake gives him an elbow in the ribs. "Yeah, Cesar's still hot for Chloe."

Cesar narrows his eyes slightly. "I am not, Jake. I just happen to think she's a cool girl. And I admire what she's doing with her life."

"So do I," says Natalie. "She's really serving God with her music."

And suddenly the three of them are going on and on about God and Jesus, and they are definitely losing my interest. Finally, I tell Natalie that I need to get back home. It's not really true, but it gets me out of a conversation that was getting increasingly uncomfortable. I mean, Cesar and Jake are nice guys and everything, but when they get going about religion, with Natalie around, well, it turns into a lose-lose situation for me.

And now it's time to answer another "Just Ask Jamie" letter. After sorting through some of the tougher subjects—things I don't feel quite up for tonight—I go with one that seemed pretty simple and straightforward, at least to me.

Dear Jamie,

I've been e-mailing this guy named Jim for about a year now. He sent his photo, and man, he is so good looking and sweet, and we are both deeply in love. We haven't actually met yet (because he lives in Florida), but we e-mail almost every day. I feel really close to him, and he wants to send me a ticket to come visit. I haven't told my parents because they just don't get Internet romances. But even though he's older than me, I know this is the real thing. I'm sixteen, and I want to secretly fly out to Florida to meet him. What do you think?

Heading South

Dear Heading,

Sorry to be the one to burst your balloon, but the only place I see you heading is for serious trouble. You say "Jim" (if that is his real name) sent you a photo, but how do you know it's really him? Like haven't you heard that lots of old loser dudes use photos of hot guys in order to lure young girls into all kinds of skanky schemes? I mean, get real. If "Jim" is older and looks that hot, then why is he sniffing around for sixteen-year-old girls on the Internet??? Puleeze. I strongly suggest you tell this guy to blow. But if you don't believe me, and you're absolutely certain that "Jim" is all he claims to be, then why not invite him to fly up to visit you and meet your parents? My guess is that he'll have some really good excuse not to. I say, lose the loser and get a life—one that's outside of the Internet.

Just Jamie

Seriously, what is wrong with some people? I can't believe that some girls are still falling for this kind of crud. Like do they live under a stone or what? I saw this news special where they exposed this fifty-something, baldheaded, potbellied, loser dude who lives in a mobile home park with his wife and four kids…and he was posting photos (supposedly of himself) that looked an awful lot like Brad Pitt so he could hook up with teenage girls on the Internet. And the incredibly lame part is that these totally naive girls fell for it. I mean, they actually thought they'd found a boyfriend who looked like a movie star. Get real.

Too bad all of life's questions aren't as simple and easy to answer as Heading South's. Like I got this other letter from a girl who calls herself Lost and Afraid. She's asking questions about God and life and death. Her brother recently died, and she's still hurting. But I have absolutely no idea what I should say to this poor girl. So I'll just bury that letter beneath the rest. I mean, the column is called "Just Ask Jamie." If they want answers about the meaning of life, they should just ask God. Right?

Now, I'm going to get real here. Besides, feeling guilty about being unable to answer some of these meaning-of-life letters, I have to ask myself—what really is the meaning of life? According to Buddhist beliefs, it is the never-ending process of suffering and self-denial until you practically cease to exist. And to be perfectly honest, that doesn't sound all that good to me. I mean, what would it be like <u>not</u> to exist? And why would that even be a good thing?

So I am feeling more puzzled than usual. And I remember listening to Natalie, Cesar, and Jake talking

about God at the Paradiso today. It's like they have it all
figured out. Well, sort of. Now I have to ask myself, what
business do I have writing this advice column when I am
clearly way more confused than most people in this
world? Not only do I feel like a hypocrite but also like a
fool. And I'm considering going to my dad and just
pulling the plug on this whole thing. Then I remember a
certain yellow something that's parked in our driveway.
And suddenly I'm not so sure.

Maybe I need to take a break and just clear my head.
And I know how I can do that. I think it might be time to
go driving with Miss Daisy! Now, if I was a truly devout
Buddhist, I would realize that taking delight in such
obvious materialistic experiences is both carnal and
unvirtuous (a word they like to use). But you know
what? I really don't care!!!

Four

Sunday, September 4

Sometimes things happen, things you previously thought would make little difference to you personally, but they just totally knock you sideways. That's what happened to me today. Oh, not that it was about me. I am not so narcissistic to believe that. But it's hard not to react personally to something like this. And when I heard the news this morning, well, it felt as if someone had dumped a ton of wet cement on me. Like I could barely breathe or walk or talk or think. Mostly I've just been crying. It's like I can't stop.

"A girl from your school was in a serious accident last night," my dad told me this morning, laying the front page of his newspaper facedown, I suspect so I wouldn't read the headline yet.

"Who was it?" I ask him, reaching for the paper.

"Did you know Tiffany Knight?" he asks, studying my face.

"Yeah. We're not like good friends or anything. What happened? Is she okay?"

He flips the paper over, and I see Tiffany's photograph and read the headline: Seventeen-Year-Old Girl Killed in Motorcycle Accident.

I stare at the paper now. "She's dead?" I finally say.

Dad nods. "It says she died instantly. Her father was the driver. They were going pretty fast when they hit gravel. The bike went out of control and hit a telephone pole. He's in critical condition."

"But Tiffany is dead?"

"Yes. It's very sad." Dad reaches for my hand now. "You okay, honey?"

I nod, but this gigantic lump is growing in my throat. "I mean, like I said, we weren't very good friends, but it's just, well, you know...kinda shocking."

My dad looks sad too. "I know what you mean."

Then I go into the kitchen and get a glass of orange juice. But I can't choke it down. Finally I give up and just pour it down the sink. Then I go back to my room, close the door, sit on my bed, and try to imagine what dying is like.

I know it sounds morbid, but it's the truth. What is death like? I mean, I've never actually known anyone who died before. And suddenly I wonder if Tiffany can feel anything, hear anything, see anything? Where is she right now? Or did she simply stop existing the moment she drew her last breath? It all seems very strange and sad and mysterious. And very depressing. Very, very depressing.

To be honest, I'm not feeling this bummed because Tiffany was such a good friend to me; she wasn't. I didn't even like her. In fact, I used to go out of my way to avoid her. But this doesn't make me feel any better. No, instead of simply feeling bad about her death and depressed about dying in general, now I can add a huge heap of guilt onto my pile too. Why hadn't I been nicer to her? What kind of horrible person am I anyway?

Finally, I can't take it any longer, and I call Natalie. It turns out that she hasn't even heard the news yet, so I break it to her quickly. Just get it out and over with.

"You're kidding?" she says. "Tiffany Knight is dead?"

"Yeah." I take in a breath. "It's on the front page of the newspaper."

"Man, that is so sad."

"I know. I mean, I wasn't that good of friends with her, but we used to talk sometimes."

"Yeah, me too."

And so Natalie and I talk some more about Tiffany, and we actually try to say some positive things about her. Like how she became a lot nicer last year (she used to be kind of a bully), and how she and Chloe Miller were actually friends (well, sort of). Stuff like that.

But even after we finish and hang up, I still feel pretty bummed. It's like I cannot shake these feelings. I can't get thoughts of Tiffany out of my head. I just sit there in the kitchen, staring out the window like a zombie.

"Don't you want to come to church with us today?" my mom asks when she sees me moping.

"Not really."

"But I can see this news about your friend is very upsetting to you." She puts her arm around me. "Maybe you'd feel better to go to church today, maybe Pastor Garret will have some—"

"No. I don't want to go."

Mom frowns, then leans over and kisses me on the cheek. "Well, you know that we're not going to make you go. But I do wish you'd reconsider, sweetie."

"I know, Mom." I'm blinking back new tears now. "But I just can't. Okay? Maybe another time."

She nods. "All right."

Then she and Dad both leave, and I am alone in our house. And okay, here's what's weird…suddenly I am feeling totally freaked to be alone. Don't even ask me why. I just feel like I was stupid to stay here by myself when I'm feeling so down. But it's too late. They're gone and I'm here. All alone.

So I sit down to write in my diary, hoping that it will make me feel better. But all I feel is this bleak sense of hopelessness and futility. Like what is life supposed to be all about anyway? We live, we die, the end? It just doesn't make sense. And why did Tiffany have to die when she was so young and didn't even understand the meaning of life?

At least I assume she didn't. I mean, how can anyone our age understand such things? I just feel so confused, and I wish there was someone I could talk to. Really talk to. Someone who gets me. But who would that be?

Oh, I know my parents love me, and they'd try to understand, but I don't think they really get me. Not really. And there's Natalie, but she sounded as confused as I do. Well, except for the fact that she believes Tiffany is in heaven. Still, I don't know how she can be so sure about something like that. How can we know? I consider calling Natalie and grilling her further on this whole thing, but I know that she, like my parents, is probably sitting in church right now.

I try playing my violin for a while. Sometimes that soothes me and helps my head to relax and unwind. But today it only makes me feel more sad and lonely. It's like the notes are just reverberating through the empty rooms and hallways of this house before they come back to taunt me with their loneliness. Finally I put my violin away.

And so I sit here, all alone, just drowning beneath questions and fears and doubts. I think about the kids who write those letters to me (or rather to Jamie), and I remember how pathetic and hopeless I figured they must feel to write to a complete stranger for advice. But now I think I understand how they feel. Today I get it. I feel that same kind of desperation too. I'd like to write a letter to Jamie myself. This is how it would go.

Dear Jamie,

What is the meaning of life? Why do some people live and some people die? Is it like Buddha says—should we give up our lives and suffer and deny ourselves everything in order to evolve to a higher spiritual plane? And what would that be anyway? And what about my family and friends who call themselves Christians? How is it that they seem so confident and assured about these impossible-to-comprehend things? I just don't get that. I mean, what am I missing here? And what happens when we die? Do we come back again in a lower life form? Do we go to some heavenly place? Or do we simply decompose and grow lush green grass? Tell me, Jamie, do you know the answers to these questions? I doubt it.

Hopeless but Searching

And how would Jamie answer this letter? Of course, she'd do the same thing that she did with similar letters. She would bury it beneath the pile and pretend it simply wasn't there. Ignore it and maybe it will go away. But somehow I don't think so.

I end up just walking around my house and feeling more and more confused. I consider getting into my Jeep and taking a ride to distract myself. But what if the Jeep goes out of control and I get in a wreck and am killed? What then?

And as crazy as it sounds, I feel frightened for my own life. I mean, I'm not ready to call it quits yet. But if

Tiffany could be extinguished—just like that; like now you see her, now you don't—well, couldn't it happen to me too? And I just don't think I can handle checking out of here yet. I'm not ready for what comes next. Even if nothing comes next, I'm sure not ready for that either. Can't someone please help me?

Monday, September 5

I feel a little bit better today. But not much. Oh, I've gotten a whole lot better at concealing my neurotic state of freaked-out angst. It's not like I plan to go around crying in front of everyone, as if Tiffany had been my best friend and I'm brokenhearted over losing her, which most people could see right through anyway. Even so, it's like I can't stop thinking about her. Like I'm being haunted or becoming obsessed or something.

And I still feel guilty that I wasn't kinder to her when she was alive. Not that I was ever rude exactly. But sometimes I was slightly oblivious or maybe even superior. And if I truly believe in Buddhism, I should be seriously disturbed by this.

Mostly I'm disturbed that I can't stop thinking about this whole life and death thing. I suppose it's healthy to realize that we're all going to die someday. I mean, it's inevitable. And for some of us it will come sooner than we expect. But really, does anyone expect to die ever?

As much as I try, I cannot imagine being dead. I don't even know what that means. And for a girl who's prided herself on accumulating knowledge and having a pretty good grasp on academics—I mean, I ace all my tests—I am seriously deficient when it comes to real spiritual wisdom. And this is really bumming me.

"Tiffany was a Christian, you know," Natalie told me after we finished running today.

I just shrugged. "So?"

"So, she's okay."

"What do you mean <u>okay</u>?" I asked as I tried to catch my breath.

"I mean, she's with God now." Natalie undid her ponytail and gave her hair a shake. "She's perfectly happy."

I stooped to retie my shoe. "Perfectly happy?" I echoed as I stood back up. "Seriously, what does that mean?"

"That she's with God in heaven, and that she's probably having a totally radical time up there."

I stared at my best friend for an unbelieving few seconds, wondering how she can be so absolutely certain. Like how does an intelligent, thinking kind of girl simply accept all this stuff? I don't get it.

"How do you know that?" I finally challenged her.

She put her hand on my shoulder now. "It's about faith, Kim. God said it, I believe it, that settles it."

"Just like that?"

She nodded. "Yep."

Suddenly I felt those tears coming on again, but we were already at my house, and I figured I could escape and get inside without creating another stupid scene. Not that Natalie wouldn't understand. She totally would. I guess it was just my pride and not wanting to look like an emotional basket case again.

"I'll call you later," I yelled over my shoulder as I jogged up the driveway to the side door. I was barely inside the house when my mom cornered me in the kitchen.

"Why don't you come to the church picnic today?" she said as she filled a Ziploc bag with brownies.

"They still do their annual Labor Day picnic?" I asked in an unimpressed voice as I wiped my eyes, then artfully sneaked a brownie from the plate while Mom wasn't looking.

"It's a tradition, Kim. You used to love it as a kid."

"That was then, this is now." I chewed on the brownie, disappointed that it wasn't as good as I'd hoped. Or maybe it was me and my depressed state of mind. They say your emotions can affect your taste buds.

"But your dad and I would like to be with you today, Kimmy." She was using her pleading voice now. "This is a family day."

But I was not to be deterred. I had no intention of spending most of the day at a park with a bunch of people I don't even know that well anymore. "Why don't you guys just blow it off," I suggested hopefully. "Maybe we could go catch a movie or something?"

"We can't do that, Kim. Your dad and I promised to

supervise the kids' games this year. It's too late to back out of it now."

I just shrugged. "Yeah, that's too bad. Maybe some other time."

"But, Kim—"

"It's okay, Mom," I told her as I left the kitchen. "I understand."

I could hear her still trying to apologize to me, but I just kept going. It's not that I felt she owed me an apology, exactly. I mean, I was the one who refused to go to their silly picnic in the first place. But I think my feelings were probably hurt that my parents would choose a bunch of church kids over me. Especially when I actually felt like I needed them for once.

Now wasn't that a change? It figures. If you don't want your parents around, you can't get rid of them. But the one time you want them, they're heading off for some lame picnic! Okay, maybe I am spoiled.

"Grow up, Kim," I lectured myself as I took a long, hot shower. "Get a grip. Chill. Move on." But I still felt bummed when I stepped out of the shower.

Finally, I thought maybe I should just change my mind and go to the stupid picnic with them after all. So I threw on my robe and dashed downstairs, but the house was quiet, and they'd already left. Oh, well.

I went to my bedroom, stood in front of my closet door mirror, and just stared at myself. With my long, black stringy hair hanging against my pale, sallow skin, combined with these dark smudges of mascara beneath my eyes, I actually looked pretty ghastly. Almost corpselike.

I just stood there for the longest time, staring. What would it feel like to be dead? What was Tiffany feeling now? Then I began to imagine that I was actually dead...and I got this horrible empty feeling inside of me, almost like I really was dead. What's the difference? If I feel dead or if I am dead, what if both are the same?

Then I lay down on my bed and cried some more. Seriously, I am a total mess. I wonder if I should seek out some professional help.

Five

Tuesday, September 6

All morning long, it's all anyone talks about. It's the first day back at school, but everyone is obsessed over Tiffany Knight's tragic death. Like, "When was the last time you saw her?" Or, "What was the last thing she said to you?" And, "Did you hear that her mom is going to sue her dad if he survives?" Stuff like that. It's as if everyone is totally preoccupied with her life, or rather death, almost as much as I am.

But I must admit that it's kind of a relief to hear all this. Maybe I'm not so weird after all. It helps to know what other kids are thinking and feeling. And it's reassuring that not everyone is as confident about the afterlife as Natalie or Cesar or Jake.

Some "normal" kids, like me, feel pretty confused and depressed about the whole life and death issue. Then others act like, "Hey, it's no big deal." Like they figure we live, we die, so what's the difference? And as much as I wish I could be that laid back, I just don't get it. And quite honestly, I think they're just putting on a big front to look cool. Either that or they're in total denial. I'm not sure.

There's a grief counselor at our school today. She'll be there until after the memorial service tomorrow. But despite my earlier fear that I might need professional help, I have no intention of making an appointment with her. I figure she'll have her hands full with kids who were actually Tiffany's friends. Not that Tiffany had so many friends. But she had more than you'd think. Or at least it seems so now. And I'm not about to question them.

By the second half of the day, I'm surprised to find that everyone seems to be moving on. And by the end of the day, it's like they've totally forgotten about Tiffany. Now everyone seems concerned about things like too much homework in chemistry, or who's going to win the football game on Friday, or what happened to the old vending machine that used to be next to the office.

But I seem to be stuck, because I'm still thinking about Tiffany. And on my way to lit class, I thought I saw her ghost in the hallway. Okay, I'm sure I imagined it. But it's like I felt this weird kind of chilling sensation just as I passed by the girls' bathroom. And for whatever reason, I thought maybe it was her. All right, maybe I do need professional help.

When I get home, I discover a large manila envelope

full of "Just Ask Jamie" letters sitting on the kitchen counter—some are still in their envelopes, and some have been printed off from the e-mails received at the newspaper office. On top of this stack is a Post-it note from my dad.

"Today's column was great, Kim. Keep up the good work. We're all proud of you. Love, Dad."

Well, that's all just fine and dandy, but when I open the envelope and start reading the letters, I feel like crying all over again. Most of them were written after Tiffany's accident and have serious questions about heavy topics like life and death and God. My favorite subjects. Yeah, right.

I sift through the stack again, until I finally locate a few of the lighter weight letters—letters I will answer. The other ones will be filed in my new JUST FORGET IT box (which is really a large shoebox from a pair of boots that I recently got). I will keep this box under my bed and hopefully, like it says on the top in bold black letters, I can JUST FORGET IT. But I'm not so sure. In the meantime, I will answer those rather obvious letters like this one.

Dear Jamie,
I've been best friends with "Lisa" for about a year. But sometimes I think she's just using me. Like she always expects me to be available to hang with her no

matter what's going on in my life. And I do. But then lots of times (like when I need someone to talk to), she's too busy. Like last week when I was really bummed over a stupid boy, she wouldn't even listen to me. It's like she didn't even care that I was hurting. I wanted to blow off our friendship right then, but I didn't. Do you think I should give her another chance?

Hurtin' 4 Certain

Dear Hurtin',

It sounds like "Lisa" needs to take Friendship 101 again, since she obviously doesn't understand that a good friendship is like a two-way street, meaning it comes and it goes—both ways. I think you need to be honest with her and tell her that you feel used by her. It's possible she doesn't know. Or she may not care. Either way, you should get to the bottom of it. Then you have to decide if you enjoy her friendship enough to continue with it, or if it's time for you to move on. Whatever you do, I'm sure you'll be okay since you sound like a sensitive and caring person. And if you want to have a good friend, you first must be a good friend.

Just Jamie

Now I am seriously thankful that Natalie is such a good friend to me. And I just realized that I forgot to ask her if she wants a ride to Tiffany's funeral tomorrow. I decided that I need to go. At first I thought it would be hypocritical to attend (since I really wasn't a good friend to her), but now I feel like I can go as sort of an apology to her and to honor her. Somehow it seems the right thing to do. And it will be much easier with Natalie sitting beside me.

Wednesday, September 7

The funeral is packed out, mostly with kids from Harrison High. You'd think that Tiffany had been the most popular girl in the school, but I wonder if some of these kids aren't here just to get the afternoon off. Okay, that's terrible of me, but I still wonder.

Natalie and I sit way in the back, but I feel it's appropriate since neither of us were close to her. The room is stiflingly quiet. Like everyone is as uncomfortable as I am. And suddenly I almost wish I hadn't come. But there's no leaving now. That would draw attention, and I hate that. Mostly I like to slip by without too much notice. Not that I want to be ignored. But I don't want people staring at me either.

Here I go on and on again, thinking primarily of myself. Sometimes I wonder if I have a narcissistic personality. I hope not. It certainly wouldn't bode well for an aspiring Buddhist. If I really am.

As the pastor comes forward to speak, I tell my brain to shut up. This is about Tiffany, not me. Then I am surprised to see that the band Redemption is here. Chloe walks up to the microphone and introduces a song called "The Heaven Song." And despite my promise to remain in control today, I am crying harder than ever by the time they finish.

Natalie is just smiling, like the words didn't get to her at all. But maybe that's because she's a Christian and actually believes in heaven. For me it's like hearing about a great party that you're not invited to attend. And now I can't stop crying. Natalie hands me a tissue from her purse, and before long it's totally soaked with my tears.

It only gets worse when Chloe begins to speak. She admits that she wasn't a very good friend to Tiffany and that she felt guilty and depressed when she learned of her death. I find this difficult to believe since Chloe was always nice to Tiffany. And that was even after Tiffany had made Chloe totally miserable during a lot of our freshman year. But Chloe had forgiven her, and after Chloe's band started seeing success, Tiffany would usually act like they were best friends.

Anyway, I totally don't get why someone like Chloe should feel guilty. But suddenly she's up there, challenging us to be better friends to each other, since we never know how long we have together. And to my relief, a lot of people are crying now. I guess it's true that misery really does love company. But at least I don't feel so conspicuous now. Even Natalie is crying.

Even from back here I can see the two glistening streaks of tears running down Chloe's face as she tells us that Tiffany made a commitment to God not long before she died.

"And even though I know Tiffany is in heaven now," Chloe says in that convincing way of hers, "and believe me, I have no doubts about that—I feel sad that I won't get to see our friendship grow down here on earth. It's like we'd been through all the hard stuff together, and it was just about to get good, but now she's gone." Chloe pauses to take a breath. "And I am really going to miss her."

Then Redemption sings a moving song that Chloe wrote especially for Tiffany. It's about seeing her later (in heaven), and it seems to be full of hope. Although to be honest, I'm not feeling terribly hopeful myself. But somehow the song does seem to make a lot of the other kids feel better.

But I am perfectly miserable, and all I want to do is get out of here before I actually have to talk to someone. Thankfully, Natalie seems to understand this. And I'm relieved that we can make a quick exit from the back.

"That was so cool," Nat says as we get into the Jeep.

I turn around and stare at her. "Cool?"

"Yeah, the whole thing about Tiffany giving her heart to God. That was so awesome."

I sigh and turn the key in the ignition. "Whatever," I mumble.

Natalie talks some more as I drive toward home. She's going on about heaven and God, and it's all I can do not to pull over and just scream. But I control myself and manage to make it safely into our neighborhood.

"Earth to Kim," I hear Natalie saying, and I realize

that I've actually blocked her conversation out entirely.

"Huh?" I say as I turn down our street.

"I was just asking if you're okay."

"Okay?"

"Yeah, you seemed kind of upset at the service. Are you doing okay?"

I nod and pull up in front of her house. "Yeah, I'm great."

She frowns now. "No, you're not, Kim. Do you want to talk?"

I kind of shrug.

"What if I promise not to preach?" she says.

I give her my skeptical look.

"Seriously. I won't."

"I don't know how to explain everything, Nat. I guess I've just got lots of questions running 'round and 'round in my brain. I'm not even sure where I'd begin."

"How's the Buddhist thing working for you?" I can tell by the way she says this that she's assuming it's not—working, that is.

"It's okay," I lie.

"Really?" She frowns, unconvinced.

"Okay, not really. I'm actually feeling like a pretty crummy Buddhist, since I didn't exactly have loving thoughts toward Tiffany. I mean, before she died. And even at her funeral, I was so self-absorbed and worried about my own pathetic life. If I ever come back to earth, I'm sure it will be as an amoeba or a flea or mosquito or something equally unspectacular and obnoxious."

Natalie laughs, and suddenly I feel a little better. "Well, you don't have to figure it all out in a day, Kim."

"I know."

"And besides, it's only a matter of time."

"Until what?" I ask.

She smiles in this knowing way. "Until you realize that God loves you and has a great plan for your life."

I roll my eyes at her. "You said you weren't going to preach, Nat."

She shrugs. "Guess I blew it."

I just shake my head, as if this is unbelievable. "And you call yourself a Christian?"

She smirks at me. "Hey, just because I'm a Christian doesn't mean I don't make mistakes. The good thing about God is that He takes us as we are. Unlike your Buddhist beliefs where you have to beat yourself up to be perfect, Jesus already took care of that by being beat up for us."

"Yeah, yeah…" I use my this-is-so-boring tone of voice.

"Sorry, but I couldn't help myself." She climbs out now. "I'll call you later."

"More sermons?"

"Nah, I just need to borrow your lit notes."

I nod. "Falling behind already?"

"No," she says with appropriate indignation. "I just wanted to make sure I was on track."

"No problem," I tell her. Actually I'm thankful to have something to talk about that I'm sure won't result in an impromptu sermon. I just don't think I could handle one more today.

Six

Monday, September 12

So, distracting myself from all the emotions that have been beating me up the last few days, I immerse myself in answering some more letters for the column. (Though not anything from the JUST FORGET IT box.) Instead I choose a couple of interesting letters that actually remind me of something I went through myself a couple years ago. All right, they're kind of shallow and superficial. But it's a nice departure from all the heaviness that's been hanging around me lately. And I need a good distraction.

Okay, I'm the first one to admit that <u>someday</u> I hope to be perfectly comfortable within my own skin. I imagine that I'll look in the mirror and actually be pleased with the image I find there. But for now it's still a struggle. Although I've made some progress too. Even Natalie would agree with that.

But I still remember the time I wanted to get plastic surgery. It was back in middle school when I first started to obsess about the way my eyelids looked. They seemed so flat and boring to me, and they didn't work very well for eye makeup (which I thought I was ready to start wearing).

Anyway, I'd read about a surgical procedure where the doctor creates folds in the skin of an Asian eyelid to make it resemble a Caucasian eyelid. I actually began saving my allowance in hopes of getting this done.

Of course, when I mentioned my idea to my parents, they were completely appalled.

"Whatever for?" my mom asked with a seriously concerned expression. I wanted to tell her it was so I'd fit in with other kids better or so I could wear eye shadow like Natalie did without looking stupid. Of course, I kept these superficial thoughts to myself.

"I just want to," I told her. Well, that was when my mom arranged for me to meet Sharon. Naturally my mom made it seem like it was just a coincidence at the time. Anyway, Sharon is this Korean woman who works at a real estate office where my mom does bookkeeping. And guess what? She is absolutely drop-dead gorgeous.

But Sharon told me that she hadn't always appreciated her Asian looks. "I had to grow into them."

Somehow I got that. And I suppose Mom's plan worked, at least partially, because I began to imagine that I might someday grow into the kind of beauty that Sharon possessed. Although it's kind of funny to think about now. I mean, Sharon is unusually tall (for an Asian), and she's willowy and graceful. But I am quite short (five foot two), and although I am slender (or so Natalie assures me), I am not willowy. And it doesn't look like I'll ever be tall either.

Now I used to want to be short. I remember being so devastated when I passed up five feet. That's because I was still in gymnastics back then, and I was totally obsessed with remaining tiny. I even played with anorexia for a short time, only allowing myself to eat green salad and Diet Pepsi for several weeks.

But after getting fairly sick and an embarrassing visit to my doctor, who was quite straightforward about the dangers of starving your body, I decided to let the "staying small" thing go. To say my parents were relieved is a huge understatement.

Anyway, as I read these girls' letters, I realize that I cannot pretend that I have no appearance issues. I mean, not only is it totally false, it's also hypocritical. So I know I must answer this letter in the way that I would want to be answered.

Dear Jamie,

I am seventeen and very unhappy. I can't stand my looks. I think I must be the ugliest girl in my school. Maybe in the whole world. Even though my friends tell me that's not true, I don't believe them. I am not blind or stupid. I just don't know what to do anymore. It's like I'm starting to hate myself. I even dream about having one of those extreme makeovers that they do on TV, but you have to be older. I don't know what to do. Can you help?

Just Plain Ugly

Dear Just Plain,

Believe me, I know how it feels to dislike your appearance. But at the same time, I seriously doubt that there's anyone (not even a supermodel) who is completely satisfied with the way she looks. But your life is about so much more than how you look. It's about what you know, how you feel, how you treat others. And I am coming to a place where I'm trying to accept that I look this way for a reason. Okay, I don't know what that reason is, but I'm hoping that it's all going to work out eventually. So I recommend that you quit spending so much time in front of the mirror and get out and do something that you really enjoy doing. And if you're having a really good time, I'm guessing you won't be so obsessed with things you can't change anyway. And remember, you're not alone! We all feel like this sometimes.

Just Jamie

Then I call Natalie (my local fashion and beauty expert) and ask her if she likes the way she looks. And just for the record, I think she is quite beautiful. I mean, her nose is probably a little too big for her face (or so she says), but I actually think it's quite striking, really. It gives her character. And I happen to think her blue eyes and long blond hair are totally stunning. Plus she's tall.

"What?" she says like maybe she didn't hear me right.

"How do you feel about your looks?" I say again.

"Why?"

"I just wondered." I pause, feeling kind of dumb. "I mean, I guess I was having sort of an identity crisis just now, and I wondered how you're doing, like do you ever feel unattractive?"

She laughs. "Well, to be honest I have this zit that's trying to pop out on my chin, and my hair is really looking pretty drab and dreary today, and I won't even mention my nose. But really, Kim, I don't get why you're asking me this right now."

"I guess it's just kind of reassuring to know that I'm not the only one who freaks out over her looks."

"Why are you freaking? You are beautiful, Kim. I mean, I would love to look like you. You're like the little Asian princess."

"Oh, puleeze, don't even get started." But the truth is, I actually kind of like it when she goes down this road.

"You are," she assures me. "You have the most gorgeous skin imaginable. Your hair is thick and glossy and black. And you have NEVER had a bad hair day in your life. And your eyes are—"

"Okay, okay." I stop her. As much as I like this, a girl can only take so much. Even so, I am reminded why Natalie is my best fiend, and I immediately forgive her for her sermon earlier. I mean, who could ask for anyone more loyal than this? Of course, I know it's my turn to reciprocate now.

"Well, you know I think you're beautiful too. I can't even think how many times I would've happily traded appearances with you. It's too bad there's not some way to do that. You know like 'Freaky Friday'?"

She laughs. "Hey, I'd go for it. I could have a lot of fun walking around in your skin for a while."

"So you say."

"I could. Of course, I'd dress you a whole lot differently."

"Yeah, I can just imagine. Do you think we'll ever like our own looks?"

"I hope so," she says in this wistful voice. "And I actually believe God made me this way on purpose. So He must think I look okay. In the meantime, I'd better put some Clearasil on this zit before it takes over my whole face."

"Yeah, you could star in a sci-fi flick called 'The Face That Got Swallowed by the Pimple from Pluto.'"

She laughs. "Hey, I gotta go. It sounds like Micah and Krissy are having some huge fight, and my mom's still at the grocery store. I think she's really out getting a massage or pedicure or something."

I feel bad for Nat as I hang up the phone. I know her life's not easy, and it's sweet how she takes the time to encourage me—especially when it comes to something as silly as my looks.

Then I pause to peer into the mirror to see if what

she just told me was really true. But all I see is a rather flat-looking face without much color, a nose that seems a little broad, and dark eyes that look as if they've been slit into my skin. Okay, I guess my hair is all right. And I should be thankful that my complexion is clear, but other than that, well, I'm just not so sure. But maybe Natalie's right; maybe we look the way we do for a reason.

And maybe we should all stop complaining about our appearances so much. Okay, I'm running low on sympathy right now, because the next letter really bugs me. I mean, this girl is only fifteen, and she wants a boob job. Puleeze!

Dear Jamie,

I'm fifteen, but my body looks like I'm in fifth grade. My mom keeps telling me to be patient, but I am absolutely certain that it's not going to get better. And now that school's starting, I'm totally freaking. I know that this will be one more year of getting teased in the locker room. What I want to know is—do you think it would be wrong to get breast implants? My mom really likes your column, and I think if you said it was okay, she would agree. So, how about it? Don't you think my life would be way better if my body matched my age?

Flat-Out Frustrated

Dear Flat-Out,

Sorry, but I'm with your mom. I think you need to be patient. For one thing, your body might kick into gear

*and change its shape. And what if you had the implants
and eventually got stuck with like a 38 triple-D chest?
Or what if you get older and decide that you like your
body as is? Either way, I'm sure you'd be glad that you
waited. Fifteen is way too young to go under the knife
for purely cosmetic reasons!*

   Just Jamie

Well, at least these letters got me thinking about
something besides life and death. Okay, so I'm having a
little identity crisis of my own right now. But I think I'll
take Jamie's advice and do something I love doing. Like
playing my violin. Yeah, that ought to do it!

Friday, September 16

I had an attack of conscience today. I was having this
great heart-to-heart talk with my mom. I mean, she was
saying stuff like how she's so proud of me and how
I'm such a wonderful daughter and all this crud. And
suddenly I just couldn't take it anymore. I was going to
scream or explode or something. I guess that's what guilt
can do to a person.

   "I have to tell you something, Mom," I interrupted
her in midsentence.

   Naturally, she got worried. "What's wrong?"

   "I lied to you. Well, not exactly lied. But I kept the
truth from you."

"What do you mean?" She sat across from me at the breakfast bar. She put her elbows on the counter and leaned forward with concerned eyes. "You can tell me."

"Well, it was about a month ago," I began my confession. "I was driving your car home from work…" I slowly poured out my speeding ticket story, certain that she would be so disappointed in me, that she would never trust me again, and finally I finished. But then she just laughed.

"What?" I demanded. "What's so funny?"

"Oh, I'm sorry. But I already knew all about that."

"Oh."

"Your dad told me, honey. He said you two had worked out a deal with the newspaper column…" She smiled. "And it sounded like a good plan to me."

"You knew about this the whole time?"

She nodded.

So now I feel like I'm the one who got tricked. Like they both pulled something over on me. I know I shouldn't be angry since I'm really the one who blew it, but I am seriously irked. "Yeah, whatever." I stood up.

"Don't feel bad—"

"It's okay," I said as I left the room.

But it's not really okay. The truth is, I feel betrayed and I'm not so sure I can trust my dad anymore. Or my mom, for that matter. What makes parents think they can get away with this stuff?

So I come up to my room and turn on my computer.

I know I should work on my column, even if my dad did pull a fast one on me. Doesn't it just figure that the first letter I open up has to do with trust issues?

Dear Jamie,

I really blew it last week. I really wanted to go to this party, but my parents said no way. So, I snuck out. The party ended up being totally lame, and I came home after less than an hour. But when I tried to sneak back into my room, my mom was there waiting for me. And she was really mad! Now I am grounded for like forever, and my parents act as if I'm some kind of juvenile delinquent. Is there anything I can do to win their trust back?

Locked Up

Dear Locked Up,

Talk about bad timing. But maybe it was for the best. Because even if you don't get caught, sneaking out only gets you into trouble—eventually. Believe me, it's not worth it. The best way to get your parents to trust you again is by showing them that you're responsible and that you want to be honest with them. Unfortunately, this takes time. But then it sounds like they've given you plenty of that. Hang in there and remember that as obnoxious as parents seem sometimes, they are not the enemy.

Just Jamie

Okay, I suppose I feel a little better about my parents now, and to be honest, I didn't really like the idea of my dad deceiving my mom anyway. I mean, they're supposed to be partners in this marriage and parenting thing. I don't like seeing them split on stuff. Besides, I shouldn't forget that I'm the one who benefited here. If I hadn't made that deal with Dad, I wouldn't be doing this column or subsequently driving my Jeep. So maybe all's well that ends well.

That letter from Locked Up reminded me of a time when I snuck out. Natalie and I thought we'd die if we couldn't go to this concert in the city. The name of the band was Death Wish, and for some reason we thought they were good. But we were only fourteen at the time, and both sets of parents had told us to "forget it."

Naturally, we came up with the brilliant idea to tell them we were spending the night at each other's houses, when we were really getting a ride with Jessie Piccolli and her older brother to see the concert. Then we planned to spend the night at Jessie's house after we got home around two in the morning. We figured her mom (who is single and usually pretty checked out) wouldn't even notice a couple of extra bodies sacked out in the living room.

As it turned out, the concert was a major disappointment. And then when we got to Jessie's house, her mom was having this huge ugly fight with her boyfriend, and no way did she want overnight "guests," so Natalie and I were forced to make a quick exit.

Of course, we didn't know what to do then. We were on foot and about a mile from home, and it was the middle of the night. We actually got kind of freaked. Finally, I decided to call my parents and confess and beg for mercy, since Nat assured me that her parents would totally lose it. Fortunately my dad acted pretty cool about the whole thing, at least while Natalie was there, but then I got grounded for about a month (which seemed like a year at the time), and it took even longer for them to trust me again. I think that's what hurt the most.

But they both agreed that they were glad I'd had the sense to call home. To be honest, I was really relieved to go home that night, since Jessie's house is kind of a dump and her mom is pretty scary, if you ask me. It made me thankful that my parents are who they are. But I do feel sorry for Jessie. As a result, I've always been really nice to her. But after that, I never snuck out again. And I don't plan on doing it now either. So my answer to that letter wasn't just blowing hot air. I actually knew what I was talking about.

It's too bad I can't say as much for that constantly growing stack of life and death and God letters. I mostly pretend like they're not there as I stuff the new ones into my JUST FORGET IT box, which is becoming alarmingly full.

Sometimes I wake up in the middle of the night, and it's almost like I can feel those letters breathing and growing down there beneath my bed. Like there's a boxful of demons, and they're screaming and yelling and trying to get loose so they can assault me and torture me for not answering them.

Yeah, I know that sounds overly dramatic, but it seems pretty real at three o'clock in the morning. I'd burn them, but that seems kind of wrong. Mostly I try not to think about it. I also try not to think about Tiffany Knight. But more and more, it's not working. I think I'm being haunted.

Seven

Saturday, September 24

Usually, I am a pretty upbeat and happy person. Or maybe just a born people pleaser. Or so I used to think. Now I'm not so sure. More and more, I'm thinking that I've learned to act like this just to avoid drawing negative attention to myself. Like I can plaster on this perky, smiling face even if I feel like crying or screaming inside. But it's starting to bug me.

I think this fitting-in thing is partly the result of being different. Okay, I realize that we're all different, and something about being an "adolescent" probably makes us all feel as if we are REALLY different or weird or freaky or whatever. But when I was a little girl and the only Asian in my class, I got this idea that I needed to make everyone like and accept me. And it's like a habit now, and I just kept doing it year after year.

Well, for the most part, that is. I'll admit I went through a moody phase in middle school. And I began speaking out more, expressing my own opinions. But even so, there's this old thing in me that really wants to fit in and be liked.

Okay, it's even more than that. To be perfectly honest, I also want to be the best <u>in everything</u>. It's like I think I'm supergirl or something. Like I have to excel no matter what. I have to get the best grades, always have first chair in violin, win the academic contests, and still come across as a "nice" girl. And it just gags me to see this preposterous confession in actual writing. <u>What is wrong with me</u>?

But what's even worse right now is this stupid column. It's like I've really gotten into it, and even though it's anonymous (or maybe because it is), I have this compulsion to do this thing perfectly. Like I want every answer to be just right. And I know that's impossible. I mean, who do I think I am? God? And why am I even thinking about God anyway? It's not as if I actually believe in Him. Or do I? I'm not sure.

And speaking of God, I'm starting to actually wonder if I've been wrong to write Him off so completely. I mean, there are lots of people who can't seem to live without Him. Like Chloe Miller. And I have to admit that I respect her, and some of the things she's been telling me almost make sense.

And yet it goes totally against everything I've been telling myself. I feel like a dog chasing its tail, going

round and round in frantic circles but getting nowhere.
I just keep getting more and more confused about
everything. And this kind of uncertainty is so unlike me. I
am the girl who always has all the answers. But lately all
I have are questions. More and more unanswerable
questions. In fact, my life seems a lot like that box under
my bed right now. Just a bunch of frustratingly
unanswerable questions.

Today Chloe told me that there's a verse in the Bible
that says we all have to work out our own salvation for
ourselves. And she thinks that's what I'm doing now.
She says that I'm on a spiritual search, and if I stay
honest about it, I will eventually find the truth.

Of course, she believes that truth is God. And when
she's talking to me, explaining how God worked in her
life, the way she came to Him, well, it does seem
believable, and it even sounds good. But then I go off on
my way, and suddenly this whole God-thing feels all
murky and confusing again. And that's pretty upsetting to
a girl who doesn't like feeling confused. I'm losing it. Like
everything is going totally out of control. And I'm just not
sure how much longer I can take this.

Like today when my dad handed me a "Just Ask"
letter. "It's from Charlie Snow," he said. "Actually it's from
his daughter." He gave me the still-sealed envelope. "She
asked that it be hand-delivered to Jamie unopened."
Then he smiled. "Kind of mysterious, huh?"

I just shrugged and opened the envelope. Of course,
I am fully aware that Charlie Snow is the owner of the

newspaper, and consequently my dad's boss.

"What's it say?" He attempted to look over my shoulder.

"Hey." I extracted the one-page letter. "If it's supposed to be private, you shouldn't be poking your nose in here."

He laughed. "Good point."

Then I began reading and quickly realize it was another one of those unanswerable letters that will be promptly filed in the box beneath my bed. I refolded the letter and slipped it back into the envelope.

"Make sure you answer that one," he told me as he headed for the kitchen.

"Why?"

"Because Charlie's daughter told him it was really important, and she wants to see an answer in the paper."

I frowned. "Are you trying to tell me that this will affect your job or something?"

He laughed. "No, it's not as if I'll get fired or anything. But it never hurts to keep the boss happy. So far, he's been supportive of the column. But we wouldn't want to disappoint his daughter, Kim."

I studied my dad for a moment. I wanted to ask how he imagined that I was capable of answering questions like this when I didn't even have the answers for myself, but I suspected that would only lead to a lecture and possibly an invitation to go talk to Pastor Garret. Neither of which I feel would be particularly helpful.

"I'll see what I can do, Dad."

"Thanks, sweetie. By the way, everyone at the paper liked your answer to the girl who snuck out." He winked at me. "I suspect that came from some real-life experience on your part."

I just rolled my eyes at him and headed upstairs. Parents! Sometimes they can be such nerds. I sat down to carefully read Charlie's daughter's letter. It was kind of weird to actually know who was writing this time. Although I admit that I sometimes try to guess whether or not the writer might be someone I know. And sometimes I think I might be close, but I'm never positive.

Now, I've only met Casey Snow a few times, like at the annual newspaper picnics, but she seems fairly shy and quiet to me. She goes to McFadden and is a year younger than I am, but she's really pretty, and she's got the most amazing head of long curly red hair. Anyway, I'm curious about her letter.

Dear Jamie,

A girl in our community died a few weeks ago. And although I don't really know this girl, her death has filled me with lots of questions. Now you seem to be the answer person (by the way, I really like your column), but for some reason I haven't seen you answer any letters about something like this. So I decided to write you myself. What do you think happens to us when we die? And why do you think some people die when they're so young? Doesn't it seem kind of senseless to you? I find myself getting really frightened over the possibility of my own death. I mean, how can I be sure that I won't be next? And it seems like it's all I think about—all the time. Is something wrong with me? Do you think this means I'm going to die young too? How do you deal with these things? How do you make the fear go away?

Frightened and Confused

Wow, how do I answer that letter? I mean, it's almost as if I could've written it myself. Her questions are exactly the same as mine, and to be honest, they're similar to a lot of the other letters buried in the box beneath my bed. And now I am feeling guiltier than ever. Like who do I think I am to write a column like this? These kids, like me, have some pretty serious questions. Where do I go for the answers? Finally I take a stab at it. I suppose it's as much for my dad as anyone. I can do this. I CAN do this.

Dear Frightened and Confused,

I know how you feel. And it might help you to know that there are LOTS of people out there who feel exactly that way too. I think we're all frightened about death and what comes next. But maybe there are some things in life that no one is supposed to totally understand. Maybe we just have to live our lives, do the best we can, and hope that when it's all over and done we have

*made a difference. Or maybe this is the kind of thing
everyone has to sort out for themselves. I know I'm
supposed to have all the answers, but I guess that's the
best I can give you. Just know you're not alone.*

    Just Jamie

Okay, is that a cop-out? I'm not sure. But at least
it's honest. I mean, how am I supposed to answer
something like that? Or any of those other letters lurking
beneath my bed? Give me a break!

I'm just hoping that this answer might work for
everyone who's written with those kinds of questions. I,
for one, would just like to move on from here. I am sick
of worrying about life and death and God. There aren't
any real answers anyway, so why should we torture
ourselves by obsessing over it?

Wednesday, September 28

Just when I think I am getting over this nonsense about
life and death and feeling guilty for not answering the
JUST FORGET IT box—seriously, I was about to burn
those letters—my world caves in. Or sort of. It started at
lunch. Natalie and I were sitting with Cesar, Jake, and
Marissa when Chloe (our local celebrity) joined us.

I was just sitting there minding my own business
when they suddenly began talking about the "Just Ask
Jamie" column. Well, by now I'm used to playing it cool,
and I don't think anyone suspects that I'm Jamie, but I

almost lost it when my own best friend, Natalie, starts slamming her (or me).

"Jamie is a total idiot," Natalie says after Cesar mentioned my response to Casey Snow's letter. "She should hang up her keyboard and call it a day."

"How do you know Jamie is a girl?" I ask.

"She just is," says Natalie.

"Yeah," agrees Jake. "She's a girl all right. And she's totally clueless, if you ask me. People shouldn't be allowed to write an advice column if they don't even know what they're talking about."

"What are you talking about?" asks Chloe, clearly oblivious about the column. "Who is this Jamie person anyway?"

"She writes this stupid advice column in the newspaper," Marissa says, like she knows everything. Naturally that doesn't make me feel too brilliant, but then I remind myself that Marissa is just like that. She's a girl with a serious attitude problem. In her opinion, the whole world is messed up.

Sometimes I wonder what Cesar and Jake see in her. But for some reason they seem to be old friends. And Chloe likes her too. I rank her right down there with Spencer Abbott, who I feel pretty certain is into drugs. But then Spencer only hangs with these guys occasionally since Jake usually ends up preaching at him, which is actually kind of funny.

"Jamie so missed it this week," says Nat. "Some

poor kid asked her about what happens after you die
and—"

"Then Jamie goes and says to just be cool with it,"
Jake finishes for her in an affected voice that I find rather
insulting. "Like no big deal, and no hope or nothing.
Man, it was so disgusting."

"Oh, come on," says Cesar. "Don't be so hard on
Jamie. He probably doesn't even have a relationship with
God yet."

"What makes you think Jamie is a guy?" I ask with
what I hope seems like nonchalance, although I'm trying
to distract them from the content of yesterday's column.

"I don't know," admits Cesar. "Just the way he writes,
I guess."

"Maybe Jamie goes both ways," teases Marissa.

"Well, he or she should give it a rest," says Jake. "If
you don't have an answer to a question as important as
that, you shouldn't be giving kids advice. I'm starting to
think that Jamie is really an old man who sits behind a
desk and gets his kicks out of tormenting teenagers."

"I don't even see why you guys read that geeky
column." Marissa rolls her eyes. "It's so totally lame."

"Sometimes it's pretty good," argues Nat. "Jamie's
had some good answers."

I suppress a smile and the urge to hug her.

"Not yesterday's," says Jake. "Yesterday's advice was
totally flaky."

"Well, maybe you guys should be praying for Jamie,"

Chloe suggests as she squirts ketchup onto her fries.

"That's a great idea," says Natalie. "Why don't we all agree to really start praying for this Jamie chick?"

"You mean Jamie dude," teases Cesar.

"Jamie the gender bender," adds Marissa.

"Did you guys ever see those old 'Saturday Night Live' reruns where no one knows whether that secretary is a girl or a guy?" says Cesar.

"Yeah." Chloe laughs. "Wasn't her name Pat?"

"You mean <u>his</u> name?"

And suddenly they are all chasing after a totally different subject. And while I should be relieved, their comments about yesterday's column make me feel sick to my stomach. In fact, I feel so bad that I eventually leave the table and actually call my dad at the office.

"I want out," I tell him.

"Out of what?"

I lower my voice now. "Out of the column. I'm tired of being Jamie."

He laughs. "But everyone at the office thinks Jamie is great."

"I don't care." Then I notice someone approaching.

"But Kim, we had an agreement."

"We'll talk at home," I say, then hang up.

I know I shouldn't take this stuff so personally, but it just really gets to me that my friends are so down on Jamie. Okay, I realize that I'm not <u>really</u> Jamie. Or am I? Crud, I'm not even sure right now. Am I having an

identity crisis? A personality meltdown? Could
something like this turn me into a split personality? I
wonder if I'll be able to sue the newspaper for my
therapist bills someday down the line.

But seriously, I'm the girl who always tries to keep a
low profile, and I absolutely hate criticism of any kind. I
work really hard to do everything just right, and I want to
succeed at all I do. Too much to ask? Well, of course.
But it's just the way I am.

I won't admit it to anyone, but I'm sure I'm a really
uptight type A personality. And as much as I hate
thinking of myself like that, I know that it's true. As a
result, to hear my friends dissing Jamie like that totally
bums me. And I'm starting to really dislike my life.

I feel slightly better when I get into my Jeep to drive
Natalie home. Having wheels was part of my incentive for
writing that stupid column in the first place. And without
the column, I couldn't afford the Jeep. Talk about stuck.

"Why are you being so quiet?" asks Natalie.

I shrug then tell her I have a headache. Okay, I feel
bad for lying, but there's no way I can tell her my
feelings are hurt by the fact that she and the others were
so harsh on Jamie today.

"Sorry." She leans back in the seat and looks slightly
disappointed.

Now I'm feeling guilty for being such a lame friend. I
know I can't be much fun for Natalie. "It's okay. I'm
starting to feel better now."

She smiles. "Hey, I almost forgot. Do you want to go to a movie on Friday? There's no home football game that night."

"Sure," I say. "Which one? I heard that—"

"I already have a movie picked out."

"Huh?" Now I'm confused. This is very unlike Natalie. If we go to a movie, we usually discuss what we're going to see.

"It's kind of a surprise, Kim."

"A surprise? What do you mean?"

"But it'll be my treat."

"What are you talking about, Natalie?" I think maybe I'm getting a real headache now.

"Come on, Kim. Just say you'll go."

"To a surprise movie that's going to be your treat? Why are you being so nice? It's not like it's my birthday or anything."

"Maybe I just like you." She gets this crazy grin now, and despite myself, I have to give in.

"Okay, I'll go to your surprise movie."

She nods. "Cool. So do you wanna drive?"

I roll my eyes at her. "Sure, you just invited me so you'd have a ride."

"That's not it. I just figured you'd prefer your Jeep to my old beater. But if you really don't want to drive..."

"Yeah, you're right."

So I stop at her house, and even after I question her, she still won't tell me what we're going to see. Then I go

home and check online to see what's playing, but
nothing seems interesting enough to be such a big
surprise. I can't figure Nat out today. Guess I'll have to
wait and see.

Eight

Saturday, October 1

Well, I went to the movie with Natalie last night. And she was right—it was a surprise. Actually, it was more of a shock. I'm not even sure what I think about the whole thing yet. The truth is, I feel sort of numb.

First of all, the movie wasn't playing at an actual theater. It was at Natalie's church. Okay, I'm thinking when she lets me in on this bit of crucial information, a church movie, great, just what I need right now.

"Why?" I ask her when I realize what's going on. "Why on earth are you taking me to a movie at your church?"

"You're not backing out, are you?"

"I didn't say that. I just want to know why you'd put me through a church movie."

"It's not a <u>church</u> movie."

"Yeah, right."

"It isn't. Mel Gibson is in it."

Suddenly I remember something about this Jesus movie that Mel Gibson produced last year, although I don't think he starred in it. As I recall it was pretty controversial, but I never saw it when it was playing at the theaters. Could this be the same one? "You mean he's actually in the movie or that he produced it?"

"Both."

"Oh."

"Come on, Kim. Don't be a wet blanket. This is a really amazing movie, okay? Just trust me."

And so I quit arguing, and, feeling like Natalie's puppet, I drive past the big message board sign that her church has prominently placed near the street. Today's gem is: "Open your heart, open your mind, open your Bible." Yeah, right, whatever. I try to keep my mouth shut as I drive around and around, trying to find an empty space in the huge parking lot.

Then we're walking through these big glass doors that make me feel like we're going to the mall instead of church. And never mind that I avoid going to church with my own parents—a small traditional church where nothing unusual ever happens—but here I am going to Natalie's megachurch where the pastor has been known to yell occasionally. Just great. I can hardly wait.

Okay, in retrospect, I can admit that the movie was well done, at least on an artistic level. But it got to me on an emotional level too. Maybe even deeper than an emotional level. I'm still trying to sort that out.

But like almost everyone else in the sanctuary, I found myself sobbing uncontrollably at scene after scene of violent brutality. It's the story of Jesus Christ's last day on earth. After being arrested, He was viciously beaten and ridiculed—over and over—and then He was finally nailed to the cross where He slowly died. It was very sad. And very gruesome.

But it's weird that I reacted like that, because I can usually handle violence in movies. I know it's all just actors and special effects and fake blood. I watch shows like "CSI" without even flinching. And I've seen all kinds of crazy action flicks with my dad, ones that my mom totally refuses to watch. I mean, I've seen all the "Terminator" movies several times over, and they never bothered me at all. I honestly didn't think there was a violent movie that could undo me. But I was wrong.

I didn't let on to Natalie how much this movie got to me last night. I just tried to act cool and like I wouldn't hold it against her for dragging me to her church for something like this. I even laughed afterward and told her she owed me one now. Of course, she'd noticed me crying during the film. But to my relief, she was crying even more than me. Anyway, I just pretended like it was no big deal.

But when I got home, I couldn't get those painful images out of my head. It's like it wasn't just a movie, but something real and living, like we'd really gone back in time and witnessed that awful day. And maybe it was real. I mean, in the sense that it really happened. History seems to support that Jesus actually lived and was even killed like that (even Buddhists believe this).

Just the same, what does this really have to do with me? And why can't I just forget about the whole thing? Really, I keep asking myself, why should I care so much? But despite myself, I do care. And I can't deny that I do.

I haven't told my parents about the movie. I'm not even sure what they'd think. I don't know if they've seen it themselves, but I suppose it's possible. Although it seems as if they might've told me if they had. Like how can you watch something like that and not tell your own daughter? Yet here I am, keeping this to myself. I have no plans to tell anyone how I feel. I wouldn't even know how to say it out loud.

Okay, I guess I've never really thought of Jesus like that. I mean, the way He was portrayed in the movie. A real live man—a living, breathing, bleeding, hurting man. And for some reason, this is just really getting to me. Like I have this heavy feeling about what happened to Him…His pain, His death…and I know it has something to do with me. I actually feel like I could be one of those heartless people who spat on Him while He was beaten. Like that's who I really am. But I can't stand it. It's eating away at me.

Last night, while driving home and trying to act cool about everything, I questioned Natalie about the movie. Maybe I thought this would deflect her attention from me.

"I thought you said Mel Gibson was in the movie?" I said in a slightly accusing tone.

"He was in it."

"I never saw him."

"It was just his hands."

"His <u>hands</u>?"

"Yeah. He's the one who pounded the first nail into Jesus' hand."

"Oh." Like how do you respond to that?

"I heard he wanted to do that part because he feels personally responsible for Jesus' death."

"That's stupid. He wasn't even born yet."

"Jesus died for all of us, Kim," she said in a quiet voice. "Even before we were born."

"Yeah," I said in a voice meant to convey that I knew that. I mean, it's not like I've never been to church in my life. Maybe I don't go now, but I haven't exactly had a lobotomy to remove all the stuff I've heard over the years.

But to be honest, I feel like none of it ever really sunk in. Almost like I've never gone to church at all. Or I just didn't get it. In some ways, I feel like I'm about four years old today, like I'm just starting to figure things out. That is, if I'm figuring anything out. I can't even be sure about that.

I thought I was going to answer some letters for the column today, but it's like my brain (or is it my heart?) is too worn out from last night. Like I've been in this long, bloody battle, and I'm so tired I can't even function. Maybe I should just go back to bed.

Later on Saturday

It was still morning when Natalie called and asked if I wanted to get coffee with her. I really didn't feel like going anywhere or talking to anyone, but she sounded desperate to get out of the house and away from "the rug rats" (Krissy and Micah), and I couldn't think of any believable excuse to turn her down.

And so we hop in my Jeep and head over to the Paradiso. It just figures that Cesar and Jake would be here. Like I need to see more <u>Christians</u>. And it just figures that they'd invite us to join them.

So I get my cappuccino and do my best to act normal as we sit with these guys. I mean, I try to keep things light and tell myself to just chill. I know that I'm emotionally frazzled and really don't need these Jesus Freaks pushing any of my buttons today.

But then Natalie has to bring up the movie, and before long she's totally gushing about how amazing it was, how she's never seen anything like that. And naturally, these guys have already seen it, and well, here we go.

"What'd you think of it, Kim?" Cesar asks me.

I shrug and take a sip of coffee. "It was okay."

His brows lift. "Okay?"

"Yeah. For a church movie, I suppose it was kinda interesting."

"Interesting?" echoes Jake. "I saw that movie last spring, and it was incredible. I felt like a totally different person when I walked out of the theater, like I would never take Jesus for granted again."

Then everyone agrees that it was like that with them too. Everyone but me. I just want to disappear now. I want to slide down my seat, slip under the little round table, and just melt into the checkerboard tiles as I ooze away. But I try to act perfectly normal as I listen to them describing scenes and how it impacted them.

But here's what's weird. As they're talking about Jesus and God and what the death on the cross means to them, it suddenly occurs to me that these same three kids have "really been praying for Jamie." I know this for a fact since they've mentioned it to each other several times. And I am, in a sense, Jamie. Somehow this thought (mixed with the aftereffects of the movie) are just way too much for me. I mean, seriously, it's like I'm having some kind of meltdown.

"Kim, are you okay?" asks Jake suddenly, and naturally, they all stop talking and stare at me like I'm breaking out in little green spots. Like I need this kind of attention!

"You look sort of pale," says Natalie. "Are you sick or something?"

I'm about to say, "Yes, I'm sick," but it's too late. I have tears coming now, just pouring down my face; so many that they're actually dripping into my cappuccino. I reach for the paper napkin and try to blot my cheeks and pretend like it's nothing. But it's useless. I am a perfect mess.

"Kim." Natalie puts her hand on my arm. "That movie really got to you, didn't it?"

Okay, the charade is over, and I simply nod without speaking. I don't know what I expect these three to do—like maybe start preaching at me or insisting that I get down on my knees right here in the coffeehouse—but I really don't expect them to do this.

Cesar reaches across the table and puts his hand on my other arm, and then Jake actually puts his hand on my shoulder. And the three of them look at each other, then back at me, and right there in the Paradiso, in the middle of the morning, the three of them actually begin to pray for me.

It is like so weird! And instead of making things better, it just makes me start crying harder than ever. I'm going to be hysterical before long. Maybe someone will call the crazy unit to come take me away. Man, this is so humiliating! And so unlike the cool, calm Kim Peterson persona I've worked so hard to create over the years. I want to yell at them to stop this nonsense, but all I can do is sit there and cry. I don't even listen to what they're saying. I just want them to stop. And finally they do.

About that time, I'm feeling like this steaming pile of miserable humiliation, but I'm trying really hard to come up with some smart-aleck remark to make. More than anything I want to lighten this whole thing up, as well as make them feel stupid for what they just did to me. But I can't think of a single line. It seems that the girl with all the witty answers has just been struck dumb.

"You okay?" Natalie asks again.

"I don't know," I finally manage to mutter.

"It's the Holy Spirit," Jake says in the most serious tone I've ever heard this guy use. "He's working on you, Kim."

And Cesar nods as if that makes total sense.

"I don't know," I say again, stupidly.

Then they all start telling me about how it was when each of them became Christians. And I actually begin to relax a little as the focus of attention shifts from me back to them. They go around the table as if rehearsed, although I know they're not, but each one tells a totally different story. And despite my efforts to resist this kind of "getting saved" talk, I am actually listening to them, and they even seem to make a little sense.

"Do you think this is what's happening to you?" Natalie asks with hopeful eyes.

I just shrug. "I don't know."

"It's a lot to take in," says Cesar. Then he looks at his watch. "And it's time for Jake and me to get to work."

So they say good-bye and leave, and it's just Nat and me.

"It's not like you have to make a commitment to God right now," says Natalie. And I want to ask her what makes her think I'm going to make a commitment at all. "But you should give this some thought, Kim. It really does seem like God's at work in you."

And that's when the tears start coming again. Only this time it's not so hysterical. "Yeah," I manage to say.

"Maybe you're right." Then I hand her my Jeep keys. "You wanna drive us home?"

She smiles and we leave, and she drives home without even speaking. I really appreciate that she doesn't talk. I don't think I can handle any more words right now. At my house, she hands me my keys.

"I'll be praying for you," she says, then turns to walk over to her house.

I am so thankful that my parents aren't home. It's Dad's golfing day, and Mom just started this knitting class at the mall, so I have the house to myself. I walk around for a while, feeling kind of like a zombie, like something or someone has sucked all the emotion right out of me and I'm this empty shell. But I just keep walking, almost as if the movement alone will get me through this thing. Pacing and pacing.

Finally I am tired. I stop in the den and sit on the sofa. I see my mom's Bible on the coffee table. She usually has her "morning devotions" in here with her cup of green tea. Her Bible is lying open, and I lean over to see if anything interesting is going to jump out at me. I mean, who knows? With the way things have gone lately, anything can happen. She has one of those Bibles where some of the words are printed in red ink, and for whatever reason I start reading right where the red starts.

"He who believes in Me, believes not in Me but in Him who sent Me. And he who sees Me sees Him who sent Me. I have come as a light into the world, that whoever believes in Me should not abide in darkness. And if anyone hears My words and does not believe, I do not judge him; for I did not come to judge the world but to save the world." (John 12:44–47, NKJV)

And I stop reading right there. It's like I cannot possibly take in one more word. But after a bit I go back and reread those same sentences. Only this time I read them out loud. I know they are Jesus' words because the heading before this section says so. But it feels as if He's actually saying those words to me. Like I cannot pretend this isn't real.

And now I am crying again. But these tears don't hurt like the others. These feel like tears of relief, like I've been out in the desert dying of thirst and blistering in the sun, and suddenly I'm in this shady oasis drinking a cool glass of water. It's like I've come home.

Nine

Sunday, October 2

I officially committed my life to God today. My parents
did a fairly good job of concealing their shock when I
came downstairs and announced that I wanted to go to
church with them this morning.

"That's nice," my dad said with this odd look on his
face, like he'd just bitten down on a rock in his oatmeal.
And I'm sure he wanted to ask what's up with me.
Thankfully, he didn't.

My mom just smiled and gave me this little squeeze
like she always knew I was going to "come round"
someday. And then we got in my dad's car and all
went to church, the three of us together, just like we
used to do.

Our church is old and small, one of those
denominations where you stand up and sit down and

read from a little black book. But toward the end of the service, while the organist was playing quietly and the sunlight was making colorful patterns through the stained glass, I bowed my head and silently gave my life to God.

Okay, I may have to do something more—although I'm not sure what—and I'm perfectly willing when and if I figure it out. But I did remember something today. I remembered how I gave my heart to God back in the fifth grade, or at least I prayed a prayer like that during Sunday school. To be honest, I'm not so sure that it took, at least not as far as I was concerned. And I got to thinking that even though I didn't really understand what I was getting into back then, and even though I never took it seriously, God must've been just waiting for me to remember what I'd promised, He must've known that I would one day come back to Him.

I think that's what I've done today. I haven't told anyone about any of this yet, but I'm sure my parents suspect something. And it's not like I want to keep this a big secret or anything. It's just that it seems kind of strange and out of character for me. I mean, I was so anti-God for a while. And I was all into the Buddhism thing. I'm not even sure what people will think. Probably that I'm a little flaky. But I don't care.

I'd already started to realize that Buddhism doesn't really work. The reason is actually quite simple—there's no way that you can be perfect enough or keep from blowing it. As a result, you have all this crud that never goes away—like a pig who's rolled in the mud but is never allowed to take a bath. You're just stuck with it. And the reason we're stuck is because <u>Buddha never died to remove our sins</u>. He was never whipped and beaten and nailed to a cross for us. If anything, Buddhism expects you to do these works for yourself. Because it's clear you can never reach the highest levels or heaven or nirvana or whatever you want to call it without becoming <u>sin free</u>. But how is that even possible?

I mean, I'm a pretty good person, but I still make lots of mistakes. Like I'm not always honest, and sometimes I say stupid things that hurt people. So how do you make up for this kind of daily crud all on your own? And how could I ever be good enough to reincarnate into anything bigger than a gnat or an ant or a pesky mosquito? How can anything I'm able to do ever equal what Jesus did on the cross?

And then when you consider that Jesus really is God's Son—and I have reached the place where I truly believe this—and that God expressed His love for us through Jesus…well, how can you argue with that kind of love? Jesus came to earth, did nothing but love people and teach about God, and yet He was brutally murdered—for me. It just kind of blows my mind.

And here's another flaw in the whole Buddhism thing. When Buddha died (reportedly from a bad case of food poisoning), he <u>never</u> rose from the dead. But Jesus did. Okay, I'm not totally sure what all this means and I still have some questions, but I do find these comparisons interesting. And I seriously wonder how I missed something this big before. I guess I was just blind.

The biggest thing is that I've invited God back into my life. I've accepted Jesus' forgiveness, and I feel more peace than I've ever felt before. I can't even explain how that is; I just know that it's true.

So does this mean I have all the answers now? I wish. But maybe having all the answers isn't that important. Maybe having God in your life is what really matters.

Now I don't feel so intimidated by my JUST FORGET IT box. I'm ready to take it out from under my bed. Oh, I don't think I can possibly answer all those letters, but I will attempt to answer some of them. And I'm really hoping that God will help me with this first one.

Dear Jamie,

I think I'm depressed. I'm fifteen, and all I think about is dying. I guess that's because someone I knew died recently. I'm kinda freaked that I don't know what happens after we die. I don't even know why we're alive in the first place. It's not that I want to die exactly, but I'm just not sure that I want to live either—I mean, if it's all for nothing. What do you think? Do you think it's all for nothing?

Down and Out

Dear Down and Out,

No, I don't think it's all for nothing. If you read last Tuesday's column, you may remember how I said that life was just about doing your best and seeing what happens next. Well, let me be the first to tell you that I was wrong. Really wrong. I now believe that God has a purpose for our lives. I believe He knows why we're here and where we're going after we die. And I think the only way we can begin to figure these things out is by inviting God into our lives. So if you have questions, take them to God. He's got answers. That's what I plan to do from now on.

Just Jamie

Wednesday, October 5

Amazingly, I still haven't told anyone about committing my life to God yet. (Well, other than Jamie's anonymous confession in the newspaper, which I think my parents understood although they haven't said as much.)

There are a couple of reasons why I'm keeping this news to myself for the time being. 1) I've always been kind of a private person, and I think I want to live this thing out for a while without getting all the feedback from family and friends. 2) After making that "confession" in the column, I realized that I need to preserve my anonymity by not looking like I, Kim Peterson, discovered God at exactly the same moment as Jamie. And 3) Okay, to be perfectly honest, there's this tiny part of me that's afraid what I've experienced might not be real. I mean, what if I was just having a little emotional breakdown or something? Although I really don't think that's the case, I do want to keep a low profile for now. And as usual, I'm pretty good at that.

Even when Natalie asked how I was doing as we rode to school on Monday—and I know she meant the thing about the crying jag last Saturday—I calmly told her that I'd had a really bad case of PMS last week (and that was not a lie!).

And thankfully, Cesar and Jake didn't bring my little outburst up at lunchtime. But to my surprise and relief, they were both a lot sweeter and nicer than usual to me. Jake didn't even tease me with any of his stupid Buddha jokes. Really, they were respectful, and I appreciated it. Lucky for me, they got into the "Just Ask" column again. And this time it wasn't even painful to listen.

"I wonder what happened to him," said Cesar. Apparently Cesar still assumes that Jamie is a guy. And that's cool with me. "It's like he had this total turnaround."

"Yeah," agreed Jake. "Do you think our prayers really worked?"

"Or maybe Jamie was trying to conceal his or her faith at first," suggested Natalie, as if she'd really given this some thought. "Maybe he or she, whichever it is, was just trying to be careful about not crossing that line. Like she could get in trouble for saying something about God in the newspaper."

Then Nat peered over at me, and I actually started to freak, like maybe she knew that I was Jamie. "Your dad works for the paper, Kim, are there rules against writing about God?"

I kind of shrugged like I wasn't sure. "What about freedom of the press? And there was an article about Hinduism not too long ago."

Before long they went back to analyzing Jamie again. As usual, they ended up arguing over whether Jamie was a he or she, and I began to breathe easier. Sometimes I can't believe that someone doesn't figure out that Jamie is really me. Especially Nat, since she knows me better than anyone. But then sometimes you don't notice something that's sitting right under your nose. You kind of take it for granted. Like God, for instance. I'm pretty sure He was there all along. I mean, the whole time I was getting bummed and upset and trying to figure out the whole religion, Buddha, and universe thing, God was just patiently waiting for me to look up and see.

I got some new "Just Ask" letters this week. Thankfully there were a few lighter ones in the bunch. A good thing since I felt the column was getting a little heavy. One of them really cracked me up.

Dear Jamie,

Here's the deal: I finally got up the nerve to try out for winter dance team, and during tryouts today, the elastic in my shorts popped, and there I was standing in

front of the whole school in my underwear. But here's
the really bad part, I hadn't even worn cool underwear
today—I had on granny panties! I'm so humiliated that I
could just die. How can I ever show my face at school
again?

    Granny Panty Girl

Dear GPG,

    *You might deserve first prize for most embarrassing
moment! But don't obsess over what happened, since
that will only make it worse. The best thing is to laugh
at yourself and expect that your friends will laugh too.
And after everyone's had a good laugh, try to forget
about it and move on. Oh yeah, you might want to
consider burning those granny panties.*

    Just Jamie

Tuesday, October 11

I finally told Nat about committing my life to God. I
waited until we were on our way home from school. I
kept it brief and didn't admit that this all happened more
than a week ago.

"That is so cool, Kim!"

I nod. "I thought you'd be happy to hear that I'm not
a heathen anymore."

She laughs. "I never thought of you like that."

"Yeah, sure. Tell me you weren't pretty worried about
the whole Buddhism thing."

"Oh, I knew you'd figure it all out in time."

"Right."

"I did."

Then I smile. "Okay, I guess you were right."

"So, do you think you'd ever want to come to my youth group? I mean, since your church doesn't have one."

Now I carefully consider this invitation, and although I really don't want to hurt her feelings, the truth of the matter is, I don't want to go to her humungous church. It overwhelms me.

"I'm not sure," I finally say. And I can tell she's disappointed, and I probably need to explain. "It's just that your church is so big. I feel kind of lost in the crowd, you know?"

She nods. "Yeah, I know what you mean. But I think it'd be good for you to have that kind of fellowship. I mean, I'm sure your church is fine, but..."

"Do you really think it matters whether I go to youth group or not? I mean, I plan on going to my old church again." I don't admit that I've already been there twice since my recommitment.

"I guess that's fine. But our youth pastor is always telling us we need fellowship."

"But what does that really mean, Nat?"

"I think it means we need a place where we can be with Christian friends, like people our own age, a place where we're comfortable enough to just talk and encourage each other and pray and stuff."

"Yeah, I guess that sounds cool." Even so, I do not want to go to Nat's youth group. As much as I love her, I have to draw the line. "Where do Cesar and Jake go to church?" I ask suddenly. Now they might've already told me this before, but it is possible I wasn't listening.

"They go to the same place that Chloe Miller goes. It's that church downtown in the old department store. I can't even remember the name of it."

"Oh." I consider this but don't admit that visiting the church where Chloe goes sounds way more appealing than going to Natalie's church. I know she would take it wrong. Besides, I'm happy for Nat that she likes her church. And her mom likes it too. And after Nat's dad left, I know this is really important to their family.

"I guess the best thing is to go to whatever church God leads you to, Kim. He'll show you if you ask Him."

I nod as I pull up in front of her house. "I'll do that."

"Well, anyway, I think it's so awesome that you've invited Jesus into your heart!" She reaches across and gives me a big hug. "I'm so happy for you."

"Yeah, me too."

"So, do you think you'll get baptized now?"

Baptized? Our church doesn't really do that sort of thing. Oh, maybe for babies occasionally, although I haven't even seen anything like that for a really long time. "I don't know. I guess I don't really know much about it."

"My pastor says you have to get baptized." She opens the door. "He says you have to do full immersion, going down under the water. It's like dying to yourself and being raised by Jesus."

I nod as I attempt to take this in. "Well, I guess I'll have to find out about that." But the truth is, I'm not so sure about it. I mean, what difference should it make to God whether you get dunked in water or not?

"I better hurry." She grabs her bag. "I almost forgot that I'm supposed to pick up Krissy and Micah from after-school care today."

As I drive down to my house, I am amazed at how much responsibility Nat seems to carry. It's like she's become a second parent since her dad left. Sometimes I wonder if it ever gets to her, all this responsibility and stuff. I mean, she vents occasionally, but mostly she just seems to hang in there. It's pretty incredible if you think about it.

And suddenly it occurs to me that I could be a way better friend. I could offer to help with Krissy and Micah sometimes. I'm not really into little kids. Okay, I've never even been around them much. But maybe I should stretch myself and help out. As I park my Jeep, I wonder where this idea has come from. Like is it God telling me to think of someone besides myself for a change?

Not that I'm such a horrible selfish person, but I suppose I mostly think about myself and my own problems. As a result, I'm mildly surprised to find myself feeling this concerned for my best friend, and I'm certain it must be a God-thing.

Anyway, I call up Nat and offer to take her to pick up

the kids. It's a small thing, but I can tell that she really appreciates it.

And since both Krissy and Micah seem to be starving when we pick them up, we stop by the Dairy Queen on our way home, and I buy everyone an ice cream cone.

"Why are you being so nice to us, Kim?" Micah looks suspicious as he catches a drip of ice cream with his tongue.

I kind of laugh. "Because I like you."

Krissy nods and scoots closer to me in the booth. "We like you too."

"And I was thinking..." I continue, but wonder if I could be getting in over my head here. "I could maybe help to watch you guys sometimes."

Nat looks as if she's about to fall over. "You're kidding?"

I frown. "Not really."

"I didn't think you liked little kids."

I make a face at her. "Well, I've never really liked to babysit, if that's what you mean. But then I had that bad experience with the Blanton brats. Remember?"

She smirks. "Yeah. I guess that was sort of my fault. I should've warned you that those boys were into matches."

"They were a regular pair of pyromaniacs. It's a wonder they didn't burn the whole house down."

"I quit watching them after that too," Nat says.

"But Krissy and Micah are different." I smile at them and hope that this is somewhat true, because I've actually witnessed these two in some real knock-down-drag-outs. One time we actually thought Micah had killed Krissy when he whacked her over the head with a wooden baseball bat. Thankfully he was only seven at the time, and his swing wasn't what it probably is now. But Krissy had quite a lump on her forehead for a few days, and Micah's bat promptly disappeared after that.

"So you would babysit us?" Micah's face is that of a ten-year-old skeptic.

"Why not?"

He shrugs. "I dunno. It just seems kinda weird."

"You guys are kind of like family," I tell him.

Now Krissy reaches for my hand. "You can be like our other big sister, Kimmy."

"That's right," I tell her, and Natalie looks slightly stunned but pleased.

After we get to their house, I tell Nat that I'm serious. "Really, just call me if you guys need an extra hand. I want to be here for you."

She shakes her head, as if she's still somewhat amazed. "This is so cool, Kim. It's like God is really changing you."

"Yeah." I smile. "I guess so."

And maybe that's what it is. Maybe I'm going to start thinking more about others and less about me. Whatever it is, it feels pretty good. Besides, my family is pretty small with just my parents and me. I think there's room in my life for more. And Nat is like family to me. Why shouldn't I get more involved with Krissy and Micah too?

I just hope that watching them doesn't turn out to be something like one of my "Just Ask" letters.

Dear Jamie,

My parents got divorced a couple years ago, and my dad married "Donna" last summer. My problem is that I'm supposed to spend weekends at my dad's house, but it's like my stepmom thinks I'm her built-in babysitter. I'm twelve and a half, and Donna has these demonic twin girls who are almost seven, and I'm supposed to make them mind while she and my dad go out and party all night. And if that's not bad enough, these evil twins tell lies about me the next day, like if something is broken, they say that I did it. They even told their mom that I had boys over, which is totally bogus. But since it's two against one, they always believe the twins. What should I do?

Double Trouble

Dear TroubleX2,

What a mess! First of all, if you haven't done this already, you need to explain your problem to your mom. And according to my sources, since your parents have joint custody, she can talk to her lawyer and have him work out something with your dad that will prevent him and your stepmom from turning you into their built-in babysitter. But this means you won't be spending weekends with your dad unless he agrees to these conditions. I also think you should tell your dad, privately, about how you feel. He might not be aware of what's really going on. And as hard as it seems, you should try to befriend the demon twins. If you can get them to like you, things might get better.

Just Jamie

Ten

Friday, October 14

The word has slowly leaked out (among the Christians since no one else would really care) that Kim Peterson has joined their forces. Okay, that's kind of how it seems, but I know that they don't exactly regard themselves as an army, at least I hope not. But sometimes it's as if they're taking a head count, and they get all excited when a new recruit joins the ranks. Or maybe it's just me. Anyway, I try not to let things like this get to me. I try to just go with the flow, and I've been asking God to show me how to be who He wants me to be. I figure He's the one who should know. Right?

"Natalie told me that you're not into the whole youth group thing," Cesar says to me as we both wait in the lunch line.

I consider this. "Well, maybe not so much." I peer up

at him, studying his response. For some reason I care about what he thinks. Maybe it's because he seems pretty grounded when it comes to God.

"Hey, that's cool," he says as he picks up a tray and hands it to me.

"It's just that my church is too small to have one. And Nat's church is so huge...well, I think I'd feel kind of lost there."

He nods as he gets a drink cup and straw. "I know what you mean."

"And I didn't really want to hurt her feelings, but maybe I just don't see the point either. I guess there's a lot I still have to figure out."

Cesar smiles. "There's always a lot, Kim. And don't worry, you'll never get it all figured out."

"So do you go to youth group?" I ask as I try to decide between chicken noodle soup or green salad.

"Yeah, but not at my church. My family is Catholic, and I go to mass with them on Sundays, but then I go to a youth group at Faith Fellowship."

"Is that where Chloe goes?"

He nods, then orders a cheeseburger from the cafeteria lady who never smiles. "Did you know Chloe's brother Josh is the youth pastor now?"

Well, for some reason this really intrigues me, and I suppose Cesar guesses this from my expression.

"Do you think you'd like to come some time?" he asks.

"Maybe." But even as I say this, I'm not totally sure. I

mean, the idea of being in a church youth group sounds kind of, well, intimidating and uncomfortable. Like what if they go around the room and ask hard questions and expect you to say something brilliant or spiritual or insightful? What would I do?

"I'll think about it," I finally tell him as I pick up a salad and packet of ranch dressing. Then feeling like I just escaped something, I head for the cashier.

I'm not sure why I feel this little resistance, or is it hesitation, when it comes to church things. It's like I'm being really cautious, and I don't even know why. But I am praying about it. I've been asking God to show me if I need to be involved in a youth group, and I feel fairly certain that He's up to the task.

In the meantime, I am reading my Bible. That's something Cesar encouraged me to do as soon as he heard I'd become a Christian. He said it was one of the first things he started doing that really seemed to change his life.

Then as I'm driving Nat home from school, she does something that really messes with my mind.

"Don't you just love Cesar?" she kind of gushes.

"Huh?" I turn down the CD player in my Jeep and glance over at Nat, who is leaning back into the passenger's seat with a slightly starry-eyed expression. Did I actually hear her right?

"I mean, he's such a together guy. Don't you just love how he encourages you about the Lord and everything?"

"Yeah, I guess," I tell her, but I still wonder what she's

getting at. I mean, I know that she thinks he's hot. And well, anyone can see he's good looking.

"It just seems like he really cares."

"I think he does care, Nat." I glance over at her again and am slightly stunned by this goofy-looking dreamy expression that's all over her face. "You really have a crush on him, don't you?"

She kind of nods.

"Is it a serious crush, or just kind of the same old he's-so-cute kind of thing?"

"I don't know." She sits up straight and looks at me now. "I think it's kind of serious."

"But you know he's not into dating."

She sighs. "I know. But I think that makes him even more appealing."

"Seriously?"

"Yeah. I think about him all the time, Kim. I mean, he has all the qualities you'd ever want in a guy. And he's so handsome."

"I guess."

"You guess?" She sounds indignant now. "Are you saying Cesar is not a hottie?"

"No, I'm not saying that. I just hadn't really thought of him as <u>boyfriend</u> material. He's just a nice friend to have, you know?"

Okay, here's the truth. I think I'd feel kind of out of it if Cesar and Nat started dating. For one thing, Nat wouldn't be as available as my best friend. But even more than that, and this kind of surprises me, I really enjoy having Cesar for my friend too. Especially since I became a Christian. And I know that would end if he started dating a girl—even if it was Nat. I mean, it just doesn't work to be friends with a guy who's serious with another girl. Believe me, I've been there and done that.

"Not boyfriend material?" Nat sounds really offended now. "How can you say that? It's not like he's gay or anything."

"I know. Just forget it." Thankfully we're on our street now, because I'll be just as glad to end this stupid conversation.

"You still want to go to the game?" she asks as I stop by her house.

"I guess." I look up at the slate-colored sky. "But the weather's supposed to be nasty tonight."

"We'll just bundle up. I'll bring a thermos of cocoa."

I smile, glad that we're still friends and that she's not ready to elope with Cesar just yet. "Great. I'll throw in some blankets and an umbrella."

"And if it gets too bad we can always leave early."

So we go to the game with all our provisions, and as predicted it gets windy and rainy and cold. But we're staying pretty cozy with our blankets and umbrella and cocoa.

"Hey, you girls have the right idea," Jake says when he sees us huddled together. "Room for more?"

"Sure." I scoot over and make room under the blanket.

"Hey, this ain't half bad." He grins like he just won

the lottery. Then he yells at Cesar, who is just coming up the stairs and dripping wet. "Come in outta the rain, man." And suddenly Nat is scooting closer to me, making room for Cesar to sit next to her, and the four of us are all huddled together.

Now, I tell myself that we're just four friends hanging together, trying to stay warm during the game, but I can't help but feel like this has suddenly turned into some kind of a double date. Okay, that sounds pretty presumptuous, but it's how I feel. And I can tell by the look on Natalie's face that she thinks this thing has really turned her way. Soon she is offering Cesar cocoa, and it's not long before she is actually flirting with him.

I can tell she's flirting by the tone of her voice. It's like it gets slightly higher, and she giggles a lot more. Personally, I think it's pretty ridiculous. But that's probably just me. I'm sure guys like it. And there's no denying that Natalie is pretty, even with her long blond hair hanging dripping wet. And with her blue eyes all wide and sparkly as she talks to Cesar, well, I wonder if he'll be able to resist her.

Okay, it's not that I'm jealous exactly, but it does make me feel sort of depressed. Like why can't we all just hang together and be friends? Why does it seem that people always end up pairing off?

It's not like I'm opposed to dating or anything. And I've even had a couple of boyfriends. Well, sort of. Nothing really serious. But I've dated, and I've had boys interested. It's not that big of a deal. Or at least it hasn't been. Then I glance over and see Jake, who is quite the clown, and almost laugh to think that someone might assume we're a couple. Well, okay, who really cares!

Somehow I make it to the end of the game without spoiling Natalie's time with Cesar. And even as I drive us home, I don't let on that her nonstop chatter about Cesar is getting pretty irritating.

"Hey, do you think you'd want to watch Krissy and Micah for a little while tomorrow?" she asks suddenly.

Now to be honest, this doesn't feel like the top of my I-really-want-to-do-this list, but I remember my promise and agree.

"It's just for a couple hours," she tells me as I let her off. "My mom has to work, and I've got to run some errands."

"Errands?" I echo, only vaguely curious.

She smiles mysteriously. "Yeah. Errands."

"Whatever." I force a smile and wait as she climbs out.

"Around noon?" she calls as she ducks into the rain.

"Yeah, sure," I yell as she slams the door.

Wow, I can hardly wait. But I push babysitting thoughts from my mind as I thaw out in a hot shower, get into my warmest flannel pajamas, then realize that now I don't even feel sleepy. So I decide to go online and maybe even answer some "Just Ask" questions.

I glance at my e-mail in-box to see it's mostly spam,

and then I'm surprised to see a post from Cesar. It looks like he wrote it yesterday, but I'm curious about what he has to say.

> Hey Kim. Sorry if I came on 2 strong re: youth group. Not trying 2 twist ur arm. Just want u 2 no u r welcome. later. Cesar.

Well, thinking that was nice of him, I write a quick response and actually admit that youth group seems kind of intimidating, and that I don't know if I'm ready for that yet. Then I send it and started browsing through the "Just Ask" pile and finally decided on this. I guess I just needed a challenge tonight.

> Dear Jamie,
>   My ex-best friend started dating this guy. The thing is, I know this guy is a total jerk and that he's just using her. But whenever I hint at this, she just gets really mad at me and says that I'm jealous. But I'm not. And now it's like we're not even friends anymore. All because of this stupid boy. Should I tell her the truth about her boyfriend, or just let her find out for herself?
>   Knows 2 Much

> *Dear Knows,*
>   *You're in a hard situation. But it sounds like you really care about your friend. First of all, I'd have to ask*

*if you're absolutely certain that this guy is a jerk or if
you've just heard gossip. Because as real as gossip may
seem, it's not very reliable. But maybe you have
firsthand experience with this guy. In that case, you may
need to tell your friend. If she won't listen to you, try
writing her a short note explaining what you know and
how you know it. Make sure that she understands
you're only telling her this because you care about her
and want to be her friend. But even so, she may end up
having to learn about this guy the hard way. Either way,
I hope she realizes that you really are her friend. Hang
in there.*

    Just Jamie

And while this situation isn't exactly like Natalie and
me, it does remind me that more than anything, I want
us to keep being best friends. Even if she and Cesar start
going out (which would be surprising since Cesar seems
pretty committed to not dating), I will still do everything I
can to be a good friend to Nat. And before I go to bed, I
plan to especially pray that God will help Nat to figure
this thing out before she really makes a fool of herself or
ends up getting hurt if Cesar rejects her.

Eleven

Saturday, October 15

Man, am I exhausted today. It was like this day was never going to end. I went over to Natalie's house at noon, as promised, to watch Krissy and Micah (while Nat went out to do her "mystery" errand). And the babysitting gig started out pretty good too.

First we played video games, and then we made peanut-butter cookies that were only semiburned. But after a couple hours, I could tell that Micah was getting cabin fever, and it was still raining outside. And I guess I should've known he might get into something as soon as I sat down to play a "stupid girl's game" (as he put it) with little Krissy. She'd been begging me to play this Barbie game, and Micah wasn't pleased. But I figured he found something more interesting to do since it seemed fairly quiet in the house.

Finally, about the time I was seriously wondering if
Nat was ever coming home, we finished the game
(which I must agree was stupid). I checked on Micah
and found him in Natalie's room. He didn't even see me
at first, but I saw him, sitting cross-legged on the floor,
on the other side of Nat's bed, and he was READING
HER DIARY!

"What are you doing?" I went over and snatched the
diary out of his hands. I don't know why Natalie still
writes in an actual diary in the first place. I gave that up
for a password file on my computer ages ago.
Consequently I never worry about snoops—unless there
are some pretty bored hackers out there.

Well, I could tell that Micah was embarrassed, but he
also had this goofy grin on his face, like maybe he'd
been reading something pretty juicy. And since the diary
was still open to where he'd been reading, I glanced
down and just barely saw a line about how Nat feels
about Cesar. Okay, it was a pretty romantic line, but I
tried not to look. Not really. And in that same moment,
Nat and Krissy walked in.

"What's going on?" Nat demanded as she saw me
looking down at her open diary; in that same instant
Micah took off like a flash.

"I just found—"

She grabbed her diary from me. "<u>Kim</u>!"

That's when I noticed her hair. "Nat! You cut your
hair!"

"Don't change the subject!" She looked really angry now and, well, that just seriously irked me. I mean, what right did she have to be angry at me? I'd been here babysitting these kids while she'd been out getting her hair done, and she never even told me she was going to do it.

We've both been keeping our hair long, kind of like this unspoken pact. I actually felt slightly betrayed, although I have to admit it looked really cute. And I could tell she'd gotten some highlights too, which really brought her already-blond hair to life. If I hadn't been so furious with her, I might've even told her how hot she looked.

"I can't believe you'd—"

"I can't believe you!" I snapped back at her, then walked out of her room and went home mad. Okay, I immediately felt bad, but then she shouldn't have thought the worst of me like that. We've been friends long enough for her to know I would never, not in a million years, read her diary without permission.

I actually think she was just embarrassed that it was opened to the section about Cesar. And well, she should've been embarrassed! I mean, if you're going to write stuff like that, you should keep your diary in a foolproof hiding place or locked up in a safe!

But here's where my day took another weird twist, and I am actually sorry now. When I got home, my mom told me that "a guy named Cesar called."

"Cesar called here?"

"Yes, is he a friend of yours?"

I nodded.

"He wanted to know if you would like to go to youth group with him tonight."

I frowned. "Tonight?"

"Yes. I took his number and told him you'd call." She smiled as she handed me the note paper. "He sounded nice, Kim."

"He is nice," I told her. I was still feeling hurt and mad at Natalie, and that's probably the reason I picked up the phone and dialed Cesar's number. Without really thinking, or maybe thinking I was getting even, I told Cesar that I'd love to go to youth group, and when he offered to pick me up, I said that'd be great.

And even as I said those words, I imagined Nat looking out her living room window and seeing Cesar's rather distinctive-looking old pickup parked in front of my house—and I was glad! Now how evil is that? And the really pathetic thing was that I really didn't want to go to youth group in the first place. I was only going to spite my best friend. Oh, man, I am such a jerk.

So Cesar came at around seven, I invited him in to meet my parents, and they seemed to like him. Then we left, and if Nat was looking (and I have no idea at this point), I'm sure it seemed like we were going out on a date.

But once we got to youth group, I was feeling pretty

guilty, and I'm sure I was wearing my shameful feelings like a thick, soggy blanket. But poor Cesar assumed it was because I was uncomfortable being there. He actually apologized, but I told him not to worry, that I was fine.

And the surprising truth was, I actually liked what Josh Miller (Chloe's older brother) had to say, and I liked the way he led the group. He seems like a pretty cool guy. Not a know-it-all, I'm-so-much-better-than-you kind of person. And I could see that he was sincerely friendly to everyone—even some of the kids who might normally be left on the sidelines. That really spoke to me a lot. And I thought, under different circumstances, I could really get into something like this.

"So what'd you think?" Cesar asked me as he drove me home. His voice sounded kind of tentative, like he was worried that I'd hated it.

"I thought it was pretty cool."

He looked surprised. "Really?"

"Yeah. I guess I was just feeling bummed because Natalie and I had a little, uh, fight today."

"You and Natalie had a fight?" He sounded incredulous.

"It was really just a misunderstanding." Then I can't believe how I went ahead and told him the whole story. Well, not the WHOLE story. I never mentioned that the section in the diary was about him. Natalie would never forgive me for doing something that stupid. Anyway, he just ended up laughing about it.

"Girls freak over some pretty lame stuff," he finally said.

"I know, but I'm going to end it tonight. I plan to e-mail Nat as soon as I get home and tell her I'm sorry."

"That's cool."

Then I thanked Cesar for inviting me to youth group and told him I thought I'd like to come back again. "But you don't have to give me a ride," I said quickly. "I'm perfectly able to drive myself." Like I wanted him to know I wasn't hitting on him or anything.

"Hey, no problem. I practically drive by your house to get there anyway."

Now this really threw me. Was he saying that he <u>wanted</u> to give me rides to youth group? And if so, why? The whole thing made me feel pretty uncomfortable, and I finally just laid my cards on the table.

"You know, Cesar," I began, feeling dumb but desperate to avoid any further misunderstandings. I'd already had more than enough for one day. "I, uh, I'm not really interested in going out with you or anything. I mean, I think it's cool to be friends, and I really love talking to you and I, uh…"

He laughed. "I feel exactly the same way, Kim. I'm still not into dating, and I think it's cool to just be friends."

"Seriously?"

He pulled into my driveway. "I give you my word. I just like being around you, Kim. And I like talking to you too. And I really appreciate that you're not trying to hook up with me or anything. It's like we totally understand each other in that regard."

Suddenly I was smiling. "Yeah, that's how I feel too."

Then he reached out like he wanted to shake my hand. "So it's a deal then?"

"Huh?"

"That we'll be okay hanging together and just being friends?"

I nodded with enthusiasm as I shook his hand. "I'm totally cool with that."

And then I felt so relieved that we made things perfectly clear; I really did like the idea of being good friends with Cesar. But at the same time, I was pretty worried about Nat. And if she saw Cesar's pickup, I knew I'd have some explaining to do.

Since it was kind of late for a phone call (my parents don't like me to use the phone after eleven), I followed through with my plan to e-mail her, hoping she would be online and we could do instant messaging. But she didn't seem to be there. So I told her I was sorry and that our fight was stupid and that I thought her hair looked totally awesome. I did not, however, mention seeing Cesar tonight, not that I'm trying to hide it from her, but I hope and pray she wasn't watching and that I can explain that in person later.

Then, since I was still one response short, I decided to answer another letter for the column. And this cry for help had been nagging me the last couple of days. I wanted to make sure that it was answered in Tuesday's edition. The letter was very short, but I felt worried my answer won't be. First I prayed and asked God to give me the right words.

Dear Jamie,
   Is it morally wrong to cut?
   Desperate

Dear Desperate,
   Morally wrong? Well, cutting isn't illegal, but I believe that God created us—and our bodies—and I don't think He wants us to intentionally harm ourselves in ANY way. Whether it's through cutting, drugs, anorexia, or whatever...I believe God loves us so much that He wants us to take care of ourselves. I realize that some people cut to avoid other kinds of pain in their lives. They think if they cut they might forget they're miserable. The problem is, the physical pain from the cut only lasts a short while, and then you feel like you need to do it again and again. That's because the emotional pain doesn't go away—it only gets worse. I think God wants us to deal with our emotional pain. I think He wants us to bring our troubles to Him and allow Him to show us better ways out. But it's also possible that you could need some additional help. If you can't talk to your parents, maybe you could talk to

a school counselor or some other professional. Because you need to love yourself the same way that God loves you. And that shouldn't hurt.

Just Jamie

Twelve

Wednesday, October 19

Natalie is finally speaking to me again. But just barely,
and only after Cesar convinced her that he and I are
NOT dating. She did see him picking me up on Saturday
night, after all, and naturally she assumed the worst. She
totally ignored me on Monday and even drove herself to
school. Then on Tuesday, after I begged Cesar to set her
straight, he told her he didn't want to date anyone—
period. And that he and I were only JUST friends. But
then she was all bummed about the nondating thing.

"Why does he want to be friends with just you?" she
demanded as I gave her a ride home yesterday.

"It's not just me. It's just that he doesn't want a
girlfriend."

"It's like he doesn't even like me," she complained.
"And I think about him all the time, Kim. It's like the

more he pushes me away, the more I want to pursue him. Do you think I'm going crazy?"

"No." I laughed. "I just think you've got a really bad crush."

She sunk down into the passenger seat and moaned. "It's not fair."

"Who said anything is supposed to be fair?"

"I mean, that he's okay hanging with you, and that he wants to take you to youth group and everything."

"Nat," I tried to keep my voice patient. "It's probably because he knows I <u>don't</u> have a crush on him. Or maybe he just thinks of me as someone who needs to be taken to youth group, like the needy new convert, you know? A charity case."

This seems to settle her down, but after I drop her home, I got to wondering if that might be true. Maybe Cesar and Nat and even Chloe see me as this girl who's still wet behind the ears when it comes to God. And it's not that I'm not exactly. I mean I'm not claiming to be something I'm not.

But this is how I feel. Like I did turn my back on God for a while—maybe for several years even—but He was still hanging with me. And even when I came back to Him—as dramatic as it felt—well, it was sort of like turning a corner and walking through a door. A door that I needed to walk through. But it wasn't like my life changed all that dramatically. I mean, it's not like I was smoking crack or turning tricks. I wasn't even the kind of

kid who felt okay about lying, and things like cheating or
stealing were just totally unacceptable.

And the thing is, I don't really want to take credit for
being that way. I'd like to think that God had started
something good in me back when I was a little kid, and
even though I wasn't paying attention or actually trying
to serve God, those things that I'd learned from my
parents and from Sunday school were sticking with me.
Is that weird?

And so, in some ways, it feels like I've just come
back to the place where I always wanted to be but didn't
know it. Except for one thing. And this is a very big
thing. Now, more than ever before, <u>God feels very
personal to me</u>. And when I pray I feel as if I'm really
talking to Him and that He's really listening to me. It's
like something really kicked into gear. And that's very
cool.

I haven't really told anyone about this. I guess it's
kind of hard to explain clearly. Especially when I think of
how life-changing it was for guys like Jake and Cesar
when they found God. I mean, they were into drugs and
drinking and sex and who knows what else. For me, it
was more like the next step. Not that it isn't life-changing
or like it's just an ordinary thing, but it was almost as if it
was inevitable.

Anyway, back to Nat. It's like she can't get past this
Cesar crush. Like today at lunch, it was as if she was
mad at him.

"I want to know what you think is so wrong with dating?" she demanded almost as soon as she sat down at the table.

"Hello to you too," said Cesar, tossing us both one of his best smiles. I'm sure he has no idea what that does to someone like Nat. Oh, well.

"Really, Cesar," she insisted. "Tell me why you think it's so bad."

"It's just not for me." He opened a packet of crackers and then crumbled them into his chili.

"Why?"

I tried to give her my best warning look, like Nat, you're making yourself look like a fool right now, but this girl was not to be dissuaded.

"I feel like it's something God has told me to do," he said simply, as if that should explain everything.

"Yeah, sure," said Marissa. "God actually talks to you, does He?" She rolled her eyes.

Cesar smiled. "Yes, He does actually. Maybe not in an audible voice, but He has ways of making Himself heard."

"And He told you not to date?" Marissa laughed. "Get over yourself, Cesar. No one wants to go out with you anyway. You probably just use this I-can't-date thing as a cover-up for all the girls who don't want to go out with you."

"Like you, Marissa?" teased Jake. "You've been hot on Cesar's trail for more than a year now."

She narrowed her eyes, then shook her head. But I

could see Natalie watching her, and I wondered if Nat could see herself becoming like Marissa. It may be a good warning for her.

"So you're never going to date?" continued Natalie. "Like how will you know who to marry? Just draw her name out of a box?"

"Maybe God will tell him," said Marissa.

Cesar seemed to consider this. "Well, getting married is probably a ways off. But Marissa is probably right. I'm sure God will show me who the right person is and what to do when the time comes."

"Well, God hasn't told me to give up dating," Jake said with a twinkle in his eye. "So if any of you girls are interested—"

"Yeah, right," said Marissa. "We've heard that one before. God doesn't need to tell you to quit dating since no girl in her right mind would ever want to go out with you in the first place."

I felt bad for Jake just then. "That's a little harsh."

Marissa turned to me now. "Well, would you go out with him, Kim?"

I studied Jake, then smiled. "I might."

"Really?" Jake suddenly looked way too interested.

"Well, I, uh, if I was into dating, that is."

"Oh, no," Marissa says dramatically. "Don't tell us that you've given it up too?"

I shrugged. "I guess I've never had to worry about it too much one way or the other." I kind of laughed. "Guys aren't exactly lining up to go out with me."

"You've dated before, Kim," said Natalie. "You went out with Ryan Schaffer for a couple of months last year."

I laughed. "And that was a big mistake."

"See," said Cesar. "Dating is highly overrated. I think we should all just agree to hang together as friends and do group things, you know."

"You mean like go to church together?" Marissa says in a slightly mocking tone. "Or youth group or whatever it is you Christians are into these days."

"Hey, don't knock it until you've tried it," said Cesar.

"Yeah," I added. "I went to youth group for the first time, and it wasn't bad."

Just then Marissa spotted Spencer Abbott and waved him over to our table. "Oh, good," she said. "There's a heathen just when you need him."

I actually think it's pretty cool that we can hang with kids who aren't Christians and still get along. Okay, Marissa can be a little overwhelming at times, especially if she's in a snit about something. But I'm starting to discover that she's not always like that. And I can tell that there's a fairly intelligent girl beneath that don't-get-too-close exterior of too much makeup and hoochie-style clothes. In fact, I think I'd like to get to know her better. Chloe has told me that she prays for Marissa on a regular basis, and I think maybe I'll start doing the same.

"I can't stand her," Natalie said as we left the lunch table.

"Huh?"

"Marissa," she whispered. "She's such a downer, and

don't you think it's pathetic the way she can't leave Cesar alone?"

"Nat?" I turned and looked at her. "You don't leave him alone either."

"Well, that's different. At least I'm a Christian. I mean, I can understand Cesar not wanting to date someone who's not saved. But he could at least consider dating me."

"Oh, Nat." I sighed as I dropped off my tray. I wanted to say, "Get a clue," but what was the point?

Sometimes I wonder if the fact that Natalie's dad walked out on them has left her more vulnerable than before. Maybe she sees Cesar as some sort of replacement. I know that sounds weird, but Cesar does have some admirable qualities, and Nat can't seem to quit thinking about him. It's like she's obsessed. I just wish she'd get over it. Cesar could be onto something about this nondating thing.

Oh, I don't believe God told me to make that kind of commitment myself. But I guess I'm open to it. On the other hand, it's not like guys are beating down my door for dates either. And I haven't really met anyone who makes me want to go out anyway.

Okay, there is this one guy (Matthew Barclay) in art class…he's easy to look at, very creative and intelligent, plus he seems deeper than most high school guys. But I seriously don't want to go there right now. Besides, Matthew probably doesn't even know I exist. He's never said more than "hey" to me. And that's fine.

Sometimes I secretly blame the lack of interest (from guys) on the fact that I am Asian. And there aren't many Asians in our school. And for whatever reason, I think this makes it easier for guys to kind of stay back. Or maybe it just makes me feel better to think this.

Natalie says it's because I intimidate guys. But I think she's just trying to make me feel better. I guess that's why I think it's pretty cool that Cesar is interested in being friends with me. It makes me feel like I fit in better. I suppose he might feel more comfortable with me because he's also a minority here. Although there are a lot more Latino kids than Asian. Even so, I suspect that Cesar knows what it feels like to be different.

Okay, I've rambled enough, now it's time to get back to the "Just Ask" column. And I just read a letter that's really sad. I'm not even sure what to tell this poor girl.

Dear Jamie,

My parents split up last year when my dad started having an affair with some coworker chick. Since then my mom started working out, and she's totally obsessed with her looks. She changed her hair and is wearing clothes that look way too young for her. And she's been going out with a bunch of different guys, and I know that she's been sleeping with some. It's like she's turned into this completely different person. She wants me to pretend like we're sisters, and she even flirts with my boyfriend sometimes. I know that my friends think she's a tramp, and I'm worried they'll think I'm just like her.

But I'm not. Sometimes I'm so embarrassed by her I just want to run the other way. What can I do to make her stop this stupidity and start acting her age again? Or maybe I should just start acting like her.

    Disgusted

Wow, something about her letter makes me wonder about my own birth mother. After going to Heritage Camp (a camp for international adoptees) a couple of years ago, I got really curious about my Korean roots. Some of the kids at camp had successfully located their birth parents and were even corresponding with them. And since I was going through one of those times when I questioned everything about myself and my biological background, my parents had encouraged me to go ahead and try to find my birth mother.

I spent about a month online that summer. I tried everything I could think of and even paid money to a website that guaranteed results, but in the end my attempts were unsuccessful. The orphanage had no records, other than the notes in my file saying I was "dropped off during the night."

Eventually, because of things I'd heard and my research, I simply assumed that my birth mother was most likely a prostitute who forgot to use birth control. That's the usual story with abandoned babies. Of course, it could be something else.

Maybe my birth mother had been a teen who'd gotten inconveniently pregnant, or maybe she'd been someone's mistress, or it's even possible that I was conceived out of a rape situation. Various unhappy scenarios could produce an unwanted child. But none of them are particularly honorable. Especially in Korean culture where traditional values are still, for the most part, respected.

I used to pretend that I was born into an important, influential family—sort of like royalty—and that I'd been kidnapped as an infant and held for ransom. But somehow the kidnappers got scared or something went wrong, and that's how I got dropped off at the orphanage that night.

However, if I'd really been kidnapped, the police and authorities would've been scouring the country attempting to locate me. And since no one tried to find me, well, other than my adoptive parents (whom I totally appreciate and love), I finally had to accept that was probably not the case.

In all likelihood, my birth mother was either a prostitute or someone caught in a bad situation. But it wasn't easy to accept this. I mean, consider how that makes a girl feel. Like how would you like to discover that your biological mother was a hooker? Or that your biological father was a rapist? Doesn't say much for the gene pool, does it?

I finally came to realize that who I am is not necessarily defined by my DNA (experts say that how you are raised is very influential too). And while I've mostly accepted the less-than-honorable beginning of my life and I try not to get too caught up in who my birth parents really are, I still have to wonder about it sometimes.

I guess reading that letter from Disgusted made me wonder even more. And I can understand how she must feel pretty discouraged that her mom is acting like a tramp. I mean, seriously, if my mom (my REAL mom, meaning the one I live with) acted like that, well, I wouldn't know what to do. It's bad enough to think that my biological mom could've been like that.

And although I can empathize with this girl, I'm not even sure what I should tell her. I guess I'll have to really pray about this one. Because I have a feeling God understands how we feel, and I'm sure He has some encouragement for her.

Finally, I feel a response coming.

Dear Disgusted,

I know it must feel horrible to have your mother acting like that. But you need to know that her behavior is NOT a reflection on you. And while I don't think that kids should have to raise their parents, I do think you have an opportunity to show your mom a better way. Your idea to sink to her level will only bring you both a whole lot more grief. And I suspect your mom's inappropriate actions might actually be a sign of the pain she's feeling since your dad walked out. I suggest you be patient and try to talk to your mom. Tell her your concerns without making her feel like a total failure. I'm guessing this will all blow over in time, and hopefully you and your mom will be closer than you were before.

Just Jamie

Thirteen

Friday, October 21

I invited Marissa to go to the football game with us tonight, and Natalie was not happy.

"Why did you invite <u>her</u>?" she demanded as I gave her a ride home from school.

"She seems depressed."

"She's <u>depressing</u>."

"She needs friends."

"Then she should try being nicer."

"Come on, Nat. Doesn't God want us to love everyone?"

Nat sighed loudly. "I can't believe you're the one preaching at me now. I think I liked you better before you got saved."

I laughed. "Yeah, I made you look good then."

"Okay, you're probably right. Marissa does need to

be loved. I'm just not sure that I'm the one to do it. I can't stand her!"

"Maybe God can do it through you."

Natalie just moaned. "You're starting to sound like our youth pastor now."

"Why?"

"That's what he was talking about at youth group this week."

"Cool."

"Shut up, Kim."

But Natalie did a good job of hiding her feelings on our way to the game. And Marissa was surprisingly agreeable most of the time. Although she and Nat did get into what seemed to be a flirting contest at halftime. It's like neither of them could give up on poor Cesar. And while I think he's slightly flattered by their nonstop attention, he sometimes looked like he wanted to knock their silly heads together too.

I'd brought a deck of cards with me (my dad just taught me how to play Texas Hold 'Em)—okay, maybe poker isn't such a Christian thing to do, I don't know...but I still managed to distract these guys by starting up a hot poker game right there in the bleachers. We were literally playing for peanuts. And before long, several other kids were looking on and wanting to play too. Then halftime was over, and I put the cards away so we could focus our attention back on the game, which we were losing—badly.

"I liked playing poker better than watching this," Cesar whispered in my ear, and I had to laugh.

"Me too."

Of course, this little exchange only earned me sour looks from both Natalie and Marissa. If I don't watch it, I could have both those girls ganging up on me before long. Sometimes I wish they'd just lighten up!

Afterward, we went for pizza, and Jake enticed me to bring out the cards again, but we didn't have any peanuts. Finally we decided to play for pennies (after Jake bought a couple rolls from the cashier). We ended up playing until after eleven, and the manager was trying to close up for the night. I was the big winner but felt kind of guilty for encouraging gambling. I even wondered if it might be illegal or something. So I donated all my penny winnings to the children's hospital box next to the cash register.

Even so, it was a fun evening, and if gambling is wrong, I'm sure that God can straighten me out.

Sunday, October 23

I went to youth group with Cesar again last night. And once again, I really liked it. Chloe was there again, and it was fun to talk with her. She's so jazzed that I've given my life back to God. She even invited me to come over and jam with her band again next week. Life is pretty good these days, and I know it's all because of God.

Our pastor talked today about how we're like a ship on the sea without a rudder (the thing beneath the boat that steers it) when we don't have God in our lives. And I really believe that's descriptive of how my life was going. Like I really was being tossed back and forth on every wave that came along.

My whole Buddhism thing wasn't answering any questions; if anything it only added to my confusion. Mostly it felt like my whole life lacked direction and purpose. But now that's changing. And I think the change is exciting. Sometimes I can't wait to see what the new day will hold. How cool is that?

I wish that everyone would wake up and figure this out. Like the letter I'm going to answer tonight. It's from a guy who's feeling pretty bummed.

Dear Jamie,

I must really be losing it if I'm writing to a stupid newspaper for advice. But here goes nothing. Okay, my life is in the toilet. I mean, seriously, it's pathetic! But it wasn't always like this. Just a couple months ago, I felt like I had everything under control. Now I feel like I've been chewed up and spit out. I was on the starting lineup in varsity football, and then I blew out my knee before the first game. Not long after I had surgery that put me on these stupid crutches, and my girlfriend dumped me and started dating my best friend. Now, if that wasn't bad enough, I just found out that my older brother has bone cancer. I just don't get it, and sometimes, like today, I just feel like giving up. It's like I'm going to explode from all this stress. Can anybody help me?

Hopelessly Messed Up

Dear HMU,

Man, you're having one rough year. But I'm sure the whole thing with football, your knee, and your girlfriend must seem minor compared to what's happening with your brother. Even so, it's a heavy load to carry. All I can say is, I don't think you're meant to carry this kind of baggage alone. If you're not talking to your parents or your friends about these problems, you might consider seeing a good counselor. Okay, it may sound like lame advice, but it's a whole lot better than exploding. I'm learning to take my problems to God when I'm overwhelmed. I believe that He can make sense out of the worst chaos. But it won't happen overnight. Most of all, I think you need to remember that what's going on right now won't last forever. I know it sounds cliché, but there really will be a light at the end of your tunnel. In the meantime, talk to someone (maybe even God) and hang in there, friend.

Just Jamie

Saturday, October 29

I actually invited Natalie to come to youth group with me and Cesar tonight, and as much as she would like to be

around Cesar, she felt worried that it might be perceived
as an insult to her own church and youth group. But I
don't get this. I mean, I can't imagine God getting bent
out of shape about where you go to youth group. I think
He'd just be happy you were going. But what do I
know?

I was somewhat relieved when Jake was with Cesar
tonight. It made this whole thing look less like a date this
time. Not that I thought it was a date. I know that's not
how it is. I just worry about Natalie's feelings.

Tonight, Josh Miller (fearless youth leader) was all
smiles, and a lot of the youth group kids were teasing
him, and I finally figured out that he'd gotten engaged to
his high school sweetheart, Caitlin O'Conner, the
previous weekend. Everyone was congratulating him,
and even Chloe was totally happy about the whole thing.

"Who's this Caitlin chick?" I asked Chloe in a quiet
voice during the break when everyone was pigging out
at the snack table. "Is she related to Ben O'Conner?"

It hadn't escaped my attention that the popular jock,
Ben O'Conner, had been coming to this youth group. For
some reason that totally surprised me. I'd just assumed
he was one of those shallow guys who wouldn't be
caught dead in a place like this. But there he was acting
perfectly at home and even making jokes with Marty
Ruez. And here I would've figured him for the type to
make jokes <u>about</u> Marty Ruez (since she's really
overweight and not exactly in with Ben's crowd). Go
figure.

"Ben is her brother, and Caitlin is one of the coolest girls around," Chloe told me. "I always knew that she and Josh would get it together someday." Then she went on to tell me about how Caitlin had gone with Josh for a while in high school before she completely gave up dating.

"Kind of like Cesar?"

She nodded. "You have to respect how she did what she believed God was telling her to do." Then she glanced over to where Cesar was standing and talking to Josh. "So, what's up with you and Cesar anyway? Isn't he still into the nondating thing?"

"Yeah. He and I are just friends. That's all."

"He's a really sweet guy."

"I know."

Chloe studied me for a moment. "So really, Kim, tell me the truth. Do you _like_ him?"

I knew what she was getting at, but I just firmly shook my head. "No, Chloe, nothing like that. Honestly, we're just friends."

"Sorry for being so nosy. I guess I just feel protective of him."

I frowned then.

"Oh, I wasn't saying that you guys wouldn't be cool together." She smiled. "Actually, I think you're the perfect kind of girl for someone like Cesar. But I know how committed he was to not dating."

I nod.

"And I really respect that he's sticking to it. I think it's right for him. But I guess it's none of my business."

"Oh, I don't know. I mean, you guys went out for a while, and Jake thinks that Cesar is still in love with you."

She laughed. "Nah, I don't think so."

"Do you think you guys will ever get back together?" Okay, now I was the one being nosy, but Chloe started it.

"No, not at all. I mean, I really love Cesar as a brother in the Lord, and I have huge respect for him. But I'm pretty positive that what we had is totally over now. I know I have no plans to go back."

Then it was time for the break to end. Still, as I sat down, I had to wonder, how could Chloe be so absolutely certain that she and Cesar were history? I know I'd have to give it a second thought if I were involved (romantically, I mean) with someone like Cesar.

But I don't need to worry about that. And really, it's kind of a relief. I think getting involved with a guy would really complicate my life right now. Especially as I'm getting things back together with God and writing this column and just trying to enjoy life. I'm glad that there's not a boyfriend around to rock my boat. Speaking of messed-up relationships, listen to this "Just Ask" letter.

Dear Jamie,

I've liked the same boy for more than three years now. During that time we've dated off and on. But it always seems like I'm the one pursuing him. And it seems like we only go out after one of his other girlfriends dumps him. My best friend says that I'm just his rebound girl. But I think it's just that he hasn't figured out that I'm the right one for him. I mean, why else would he keep coming back to me all the time? All totaled, I'm sure that he's dated me more than any other girl. Shouldn't that mean something? My best friend says that he's just using me. And I'll admit that sex comes into the picture a lot. But even so, I think he really loves me, and I feel lost without him. What do you think?

Rebound Girl

Dear Rebound Girl,

You should be thankful to have such an observant best friend. And I'm with her. I think this guy is using you, and the sooner you figure that out, the better off you'll be. Not only that, but it's like you've trained him to take advantage of you. I mean, every time he's between girlfriends, there you are just waiting for him. I don't want to sound mean, but that's what I call EASY. It sounds like this guy is a jerk, and you need to get over him. You may think you feel lost without him, but I think you're just plain lost. You should respect yourself enough to realize that you don't need a boyfriend to make you a complete person. Lose the loser and get a life!

Just Jamie

Okay, maybe that was a bit harsh, but this chick had it coming. I really wanted to mention something about

God, but just yesterday, my dad told me to be careful about using God for every answer. Now I think that's ridiculous, because more and more I'm thinking that God really is the answer to all our questions. Just the same, I tried to get what he was saying.

"Why, Dad?" I asked.

"The newspaper doesn't want to sound like it's forcing one kind of religion onto everyone."

"Oh."

"Personally, I wouldn't mind." He smiled. "But maybe just lighten it up a little."

"I still plan to pray about my answers," I warned him.

"I don't blame you, Kim. I think that's the best way to go."

So I'm trying not to come across as too preachy. But at the same time, I don't want to sound heartless or mean. I guess it wouldn't hurt to look at my response to Rebound Girl one more time before I submit it. And maybe I should offer her some kind of warning about STDs.

Fourteen

Thursday, November 3

Marissa has art with me, and we started sitting together a couple of weeks ago. It was about the same time I gave my heart to the Lord actually. And for some reason (I suspect it's God), I've really started to care about this girl. Oh, I'm well aware that she has a big chip on her shoulder, but I think she's really searching too.

Of course, Nat gets irritated at me for hanging with Marissa at all. But I think that might be a simple case of jealousy. Probably twofold since Nat's not only protective of our friendship, but she also knows that Marissa has as much of a crush on Cesar as Nat does. Although, Nat's not admitting this to anyone, well, anyone besides me.

"What made you decide to take art this year?" Marissa asked me today.

"I don't know. I guess I wanted to try something different."

"Well, you seem to be pretty good at it." She peered down at the charcoal sketch I was working on. "But then what else is new? You seem to be good at everything you do. It's not fair."

I just shrugged, then looked over at her sketch. It was kind of murky and flat, but I didn't want to criticize. "Maybe it's an Asian thing," I told her in what I hope sounded like a joking voice.

Marissa nodded. "Yeah, maybe so."

I've been trying to come up with a creative way to tell Marissa about how I recommitted my life to God, but I want to be really careful not to preach at her. She gets preached at a lot and seems to really resent it. And I also remember how I felt just like that myself not too long ago. But I've been praying that God will give me the words.

"I think that Matthew Barclay likes you," Marissa said after he passed by our table and made a positive comment about my sketch.

"Why?" I asked.

"I can just tell." I followed Marissa's gaze back over to where Matthew went to sit at his table. For some reason he always sits alone. "Don't you think he's handsome?"

I nodded. "He reminds me of Ashton Kutcher."

"Yeah. That's who it is. I've been trying to think of who he looked like."

"But he's more of a serious Ashton Kutcher, you know? Not like the dork he plays on 'That '70s Show.'"

"I wonder why he's so shy."

"Oh, I don't think he's shy, really," I said. "I think he's just mature for his age. Like he doesn't want to get into all the regular high school stupidity. Plus, he's really into his art."

"He's such a good artist." The way Marissa said this, almost gushy, made me wonder if she could actually be getting a crush on Matthew now. Not that I'd blame her, since he's in the same category of good looking as Cesar. But even so, I think I felt a tiny twinge of jealousy, and maybe that was what gave me the nerve to do what I did next.

"He is a good artist," I agreed. "And since he made a nice comment about my piece, I think I'll go return the favor." And then I stood up and walked to the back of the room where I stood for a moment just looking at his charcoal sketch. He was working from a photo of an old man sitting on a bench, but his sketch took the image to a whole new level.

"You need something?" he finally said.

"No…" I slowly shook my head. "Man, Matthew, that is really, really good."

He looked up and smiled at me. And when he smiled, I felt something inside of me starting to melt. "Thanks, Kim."

"Seriously, Matthew. This is really good. I mean, hanging-in-a-gallery kind of good." I actually put my hand on his shoulder now. "Do you realize how amazing this is?"

He looked back down at his sketch and just

shrugged. "I guess it's harder to see it for yourself." He pointed to the man's back. "Like all I can see is that it looks as if he's got a board under his coat. I didn't get the slump of his shoulders quite right."

"Maybe, but you really got the expression of his face. And the mood of the weather, the dark clouds, the feeling of rain. It's like I'm there."

"Cool." He smiled again.

"Guess I better get back."

I felt slightly stunned as I walked back to our table. I know it was partially because his art was really that good, but it was also because of the way he seemed to warm up to me. I guess I was equally amazed at myself and that it was that easy to start something.

Okay, I'll admit that I didn't really know that I'd started anything, I mean, besides a conversation. Not for sure anyway. But when class was over, Matthew asked me if I wanted to get a cup of coffee with him after school. Of course, I said yes.

"You're what?" demanded Natalie as I was quickly dropping her off at home.

"I'm meeting Matthew Barclay at the Paradiso for coffee."

"When did this happen?"

"When did what happen?"

"You and Matthew?"

"It's not me and Matthew, Nat. We just talked a little in art, and he asked me to meet him for coffee. That's all."

"But you look like it's more than that, Kim. You look all smiley and happy. Do you have a crush on him?"

I shook my head. "No. I mean, he's good looking and a great artist, but that's about all I know about him."

"He's <u>not</u> a Christian."

"How do you know?"

"I know."

"Well, neither was I a few weeks ago. That doesn't really bother me."

"It should."

I sighed as I pulled in front of her house. "It must be nice to have all the answers, Nat."

She frowned at me. "I'm not saying <u>that</u>."

"What are you saying?"

"Just that I care about you, Kim. And I don't want to see you getting hurt by someone who doesn't know the Lord."

I laughed. Did that mean it would be better to be hurt by someone who knew the Lord? "Well, don't worry. I'm sure that having coffee with Matthew should be relatively painless."

And it was. We sat and visited about all kinds of things for more than an hour. I couldn't believe how many interests we had in common. I was also impressed with how intelligent he is. Why hadn't we gotten to know each other sooner?

"I'm glad we finally got to talk," Matthew says as things were gearing down.

"Finally?"

"Yeah. I've been meaning to get to know you for a while."

"Really? Why?"

"You just seemed interesting to me. I like that you're into music, and everyone knows you're smart. And then you started taking art and actually showed some talent. Well, I got to thinking this is a girl I should get to know."

I smiled. "Cool."

"It's like I've just realized that this is my last year in high school, and I've mostly kept to myself, you know?"

"I've noticed."

"To be honest, I think I've looked down on people. Or maybe that was just my way of avoiding relationships."

I nodded. "I think I've done the exact same thing."

"Well, before this year started, I'd been thinking I should change that about myself. Like maybe I should lighten up a little and actually try to enjoy my senior year before it's all just a bad memory."

"I think that's a great idea."

He smiled again, and for the second time today, I felt myself melting a bit. "Thanks for meeting me here, Kim."

"Thank you."

"Can we keep this thing going, do you think?"

I kind of shrugged, unsure as to what he meant by this thing. "I don't know why not."

"Cool. I guess I'll see you tomorrow then."

And that was it. He didn't ask me to elope with him

or to have his baby. He didn't even ask me to meet him for coffee again. As I drove myself home, I had to wonder what Nat was so freaked about. In some ways, I was slightly disappointed. Oh, not by Matthew. Matthew is wonderful, but I'd actually hoped he might've asked me out or something. I'm not totally sure. But I do think he is one of the coolest guys I've met.

Yet at the same time I want to be careful. I do NOT want to start acting like Natalie or even Marissa. I hate when girls turn into mush over guys. I think it's degrading and unappealing, and I really don't ever want to go there myself.

The fact is, I've never fallen for a guy before. Not really. I suppose to be completely truthful, this has worried me some. Like what if I never meet a guy who I feel like that about? But I'm not even seventeen yet. There should be plenty of time. Right?

Suddenly I am wondering if this is going to be it. Is this going to be the first time that Kim Peterson falls for a guy? And right on the heels of that question, what if Matthew is only interested in a friendship?

I mean, that's one of the things Cesar said that he really likes about me—how easy I am to hang with just as a friend. So I am feeling slightly freaked—like what if that's all any guy ever sees in me? What if they all just think I'm the kind of girl they should be friends with? Nothing more. And this reminds me of a letter that I got this week. Maybe I'll learn something about myself if I answer it.

Dear Jamie,

   I am seventeen, and I've never had a boyfriend. I used to think that was because I've always been kind of a tomboy, and I'm into sports, and a lot of guys just think of me as their "good buddy." And that's not so bad. But there's this one guy who I've really liked ever since I was a sophomore. We talk and joke around and basically enjoy being together. But he's never once asked me out on a date. He's dated other girls, and he even tells me about it. Usually he ends up breaking up with them because they're too clingy or too shallow or too whatever. And even though he tells me how much he appreciates that I'm not like that, he never asks me out. Now I am starting to question if there's something wrong with me. Is there a reason guys aren't attracted to me? I even start to wonder if I'm gay, although I'm not attracted to girls. What should I do?

   Unhappy Tomboy

Dear Tomboy,

   First of all, I think you should be really thankful that you know how to be friends with guys. Lots of girls don't get this at all. You're lucky that you do, and believe me, guys really appreciate it. Now how to get guys to see you as something more than a buddy? Several things come to mind. 1) You could just tell this guy that you like him, but that might backfire. 2) You could talk to a trustworthy girlfriend and ask her if there's something you're doing that's sending the wrong

message. 3) You could look in the mirror and see if
there's some way to change your image from tomboy to
chick—like maybe a different hairstyle or clothing that
brings out your feminine side. Because there's nothing
wrong with looking like a girl, and most guys like it.
4) Continue as you're doing, but don't complain if it
doesn't get you the results you want.

    Just Jamie

Okay, even as I wrote this I wondered if I needed to
take my own advice. Still, I wasn't sure, and I knew
without a doubt that I wasn't going to tell Matthew that I
really like him and that I hope he'll ask me out. I'm not
that desperate—or stupid. But I decided to call Natalie.

"Do you think guys think I'm attractive?" I asked her
right off.

"What?" Of course, she would start laughing.

"I'm serious, Nat. Do you think I do enough to show
my feminine side? I mean, you just got your hair cut and
highlighted, and you've been looking so great lately.
Maybe I should do something too…"

"What do you mean? Are you thinking about cutting
and highlighting your hair? I don't know if that would
look so great on you. And besides, your hair is so pretty
the way it is, all glossy and straight."

"But do you think there's something I could do to
look different?" I try again. "So that guys would see me
as more than just a friend? It seems like that's usually
what happens. Guys don't—"

"Is this about Matthew?"

"Maybe. But it's really about guys in general, Nat. I mean, think about it, how many guys have ever really seen me as girlfriend material?"

"You and me both."

"You've gone out with lots of guys, Nat."

"Maybe, but never any guy who I really liked."

"But guys like you, Nat. They seem to be attracted to you. If you could get your eyes off of Cesar long enough, you'd see that guys are looking at you."

"Really?" She sounds interested. "Who?"

"I don't know. Anyway, this conversation was supposed to be about me."

"It's all about you," she teased.

"Yeah, this time it is. Tell me the truth, Nat. Do I need some kind of makeover? Or should I act differently? Or do I need to write a letter to 'Just Ask Jamie'?"

She laughed. "That's what you should do."

"Fine." Now I was ready to hang up.

"No, wait a minute, Kim. You want my serious take on you?"

"That's why I called."

"Okay, I guess you don't really play up your looks much."

"Maybe I don't know how."

"Or maybe you don't care. That's what it usually seems like. Have you ever seen that show 'What Not to Wear'?"

"No."

"They take people with no fashion sense and give them makeovers. I've considered sending in your name."

"Thanks a lot."

"Well, it's like you don't care, Kim. I mean, even when we shop, you usually just buy the same kinds of things. Boring sweatshirts, ordinary jeans, you know, your comfort zone clothes. And your hair...you've been wearing it pulled back in a ponytail for years. Don't you think it's time for a fresh look?"

Suddenly I'm not sure whether to be hurt or relieved. "So are you saying there's hope for me?" I ask meekly. "Do you really think I could improve my looks?"

"Haven't I said this a million times, Kim? Don't you remember how I nagged you before school started? Every time we went shopping, I tried to get you to try new things, but would you?"

"I figured they'd look silly on me. You can wear lots of things because you're tall, Nat. I have to be careful."

"Too careful, if you ask me."

"Right. And I guess I did."

"So, do you want to do it then?"

"Do what?"

"A makeover."

I considered this. What exactly was it that suddenly made me feel desperate enough to consider taking her up on this? Then I remembered Matthew. "Yeah, maybe so," I finally said.

"So when do we start?"

"This weekend?" I managed to mutter.

"Sounds great. And my mom doesn't have to work so that gives us all day Saturday. This is going to be awesome!"

"Yeah, fun." Okay, so my voice was less than enthusiastic. But this whole thing's a little frightening.

"God wants us to make the most of ourselves," she added.

I considered this, but wasn't sure. "Yeah, well, I think I'll still write that letter to 'Just Ask,'" I said in a teasing tone.

"Maybe you should do that. See what she tells you to do."

"She?"

"Yeah, he, she, whatever."

And so it's settled. Nat and I will hit the mall on Saturday and I will try to be open to her suggestions. Who knows, I might even consider cutting my hair, but I'm not so sure. Maybe just a different style. We'll see.

Okay, maybe I am doing this for all the wrong reasons. Or maybe not. It might be that I've been changing on the inside lately, and now I want to change on the outside too. Really, what's wrong with that?

Fifteen

Saturday, November 5

Natalie's makeover is complete. Whether it's a success or not remains to be seen. I'm not even sure what I think yet, although my parents seemed to approve, and my mom was relieved that I actually wanted to buy some "school clothes" as she put it, since I've never been into that sort of thing. Mostly I think they were relieved that Nat didn't encourage me to buy anything too whacked or anything that revealed my belly button.

My parents have a serious phobia about seeing anyone's midriff. Well, unless it's on a beach, that is. For some reason they're okay with that. To be honest, I'm just as happy not to go around exposing my belly anyway. Not that it's bad looking, mind you; it's really not. Still, having your belly hanging out just seems a little trashy to me. Or maybe it's just so yesterday.

Or maybe the truth is that I'm too traditional to dress like Paris Hilton or Nicole Richie (both those girls seriously irritate me!). In other words, you could say my taste in clothes leans more toward conservative—or preppie or sensible or just plain old lady. Or in Nat's words, "fashion impaired."

"Don't even <u>look</u> at those jeans," she told me in a bossy voice. We were at the Gap, one of the few places I can usually find something I like. "You already have several pairs just like that, Kim. It's all you ever wear."

"But I like jeans."

"Fine. I'm not saying there's anything wrong with jeans, but how about a different style? Get out of the box."

So I allowed her to pick out things I wouldn't normally try. And to my surprise, they didn't look that bad. Okay, some of them were real loserville. But sometimes she'd find something pretty cool.

"I want you try on some of these." She appeared at the dressing room door with an armful of sweaters and shirts in colors and patterns I would never dream of wearing.

"I don't know…"

Of course, she gave me her look and then actually growled. "We've got to get you out of those pathetic-looking hoodies, Kim. It's like you're addicted or something."

"Whatever." I rolled my eyes as I relieved her of the pile and continued trying things on. And once again, she was right about a few things. Not everything. But I did begin to realize that I really can wear a few unexpected colors. Like who would've thought?

By the time we were done clothes shopping, Nat talked me into several things, including a PINK sweater. Now really, I've never considered myself a pink sort of girl, but Nat insisted it looked beautiful on me. And the salesgirl agreed, but then why shouldn't she, since she's there to push threads?

Then we went over to Splitting Hairs. Natalie had already set up a hair appointment for me at the same place where she'd gotten hers done just a couple weeks ago. "April is really good," she assured me as we went into the brightly lit salon.

But I was already feeling nervous. I mean I haven't had anything but split-end trims for like the past six years. "Do I really want to do this?" I asked Nat as I held back, waiting by the entrance and considering just bolting.

"It's totally up to you," she told me. "Just remember you're the one who said you wanted something different."

"But you said you liked my hair…"

"I do. You have gorgeous hair, Kim. Hair to kill for. But you could look so hot in another style."

I considered this, and suddenly I was sitting in a chair and April was combing out my hair. "Your hair is gorgeous." She held it up then let it drop over my shoulders like a black waterfall.

I nodded, almost unable to speak.

"But it's quite long." She drew her brows together as she studied me. "And you're pretty tiny."

"And she always wears it pulled back." Natalie reached over now and pulled my hair back like it was in a ponytail. "And then all you see is her face, and it makes it look like her ears stick out like a monkey."

"What?" I looked at my ears and was surprised to notice they did resemble a chimpanzee. "Thanks a lot, Nat. Why don't you tell us how you really feel?"

Natalie laughed. "Hey, you asked for my help."

"What if we cut your hair so it still felt sort of long, but not so long that you always want to pull it back?" suggested April.

I shrugged, still staring at my monkey ears which had now grown slightly red and even larger.

"Do you trust me?" asked April, bending down to look directly into my face. I glanced nervously over at Natalie, then noticed once again how great her hair looked.

"Sure, you did a good job with Nat's hair."

So I decided to just close my eyes and wait. I tried not to think about anything as April's scissors went snip, snip, snip. Then after what seemed like hours, she finally told me to look.

Okay, at first I was pretty shocked to see my long hair gone. But then I took a closer look and realize that what she'd done really framed my face. She cut my hair into layers. But not those nice and neat kinds of layers.

She made it sort of choppy and cool looking. I gave my head a shake to watch it move. "I like it."

"You do?" Natalie's eyes were huge, like she was all worried that I was about to have a huge panic attack.

"Yeah. Why not?" I said calmly. "Don't you like it?"

She sighed. "I totally like it. It's just so different, you know? I was kinda worried you might not like it."

"But it looks cool on you," April said as she removed the haircutting cape. "<u>Très chic</u>."

I smiled. "I like it."

Next Natalie insisted we go to the makeup counter at Nordstrom. And even though it was her idea, I was actually getting into this whole scene. No more arguing from me.

"This is so fun," said Nat. "Just like being on one of those reality shows, like 'Trading Faces.'"

"'Trading Faces?'" I laughed. "Is that for real?"

She nodded as she held up a lip color that might work for her, but didn't seem like anything I would wear. I kept wandering from one cosmetic section to the next, unsure of what I was even looking for. I finally lost Nat to this woman who was wearing sparkling lavender eye shadow that I thought looked pretty cheesy—although I suspect Nat may be able to pull it off.

That's when I decided to look for a sales clerk who had on the kind of makeup I might be comfortable with. This was my very own idea and quite brilliant if I do say so myself. I ended up at the Clinique counter with a college-aged Asian woman named Nichol. Her makeup seemed soft and natural looking, with a very light touch, and she seemed to know exactly what would be best for me. Thankfully, Natalie agreed too. Even though she'd gotten some of that sparkling stuff for herself. To each her own.

It was after four by the time we left the mall, and I was totally exhausted, not to mention nearly broke. It was a good thing my parents offered me some extra money for this little spending spree. In fact, they were so supportive of this whole thing, it almost made me wonder if they hadn't gotten together with Natalie in the first place.

"Wow, you look awesome," Nat said after we got up to my room and I started trying on some of my new purchases together with my new hairstyle and makeup. "You're like a totally new woman."

And I couldn't help but think maybe she was right. Although I felt kind of strange too. No more hiding beneath baggy jeans and hoodies. Not that my new look was over the top or anything. I mean in a way it's still pretty conservative. Only a little more interesting, I guess.

Natalie made me go downstairs to show off her hard work. "You look beautiful, Kim," my mom told me as I attempted a runway turn while wearing my favorite outfit—the one with the PINK sweater. Go figure.

"Let me take a picture!" my mom exclaimed suddenly, making me feel like I was back in grade school again.

So, feeling slightly idiotic and nerdish, I stood in front

of the fireplace, posing like a fashion model while my overly zealous mom took some photos of me.

"I hope this doesn't go to her head," teased Natalie.

"Don't worry," my mom assured her. "Kim is the least vain person I know."

"Don't be so sure," I admitted as I caught a glimpse of myself in the mirror above the mantel. "Maybe I just know how to conceal it."

Mom smiled with approval. "That's what makes you such a lady."

Well, I don't know about that, but I do feel a lot more feminine now. And I guess I'm curious if anyone else will notice my little transformation. To be honest, I'm feeling a little uncomfortable too. I mean, it's not like it's ever been my goal to draw attention to myself.

But seriously, I keep telling myself, my little "makeover" only makes me look more like most of the other girls at my school, as far as clothes and makeup goes. I'm still petite and Asian. And with regard to my appearance and compared to others, I still lean toward the traditional styles. It's just that I no longer blend so perfectly with the walls anymore.

My first opportunity to try out my "new look" was at youth group that same night. And the reactions were mixed. Cesar didn't seem to really like it that much, or at least he didn't say anything complimentary. For some reason this made me feel bad. But then Jake made up for it when he told me I looked like a babe. Even so, I think the best compliment I got was from Chloe.

"Kim!" she grabbed me by both hands when she saw me. "You look so awesome!"

"Really, you like it?"

"I love it. That haircut is perfect."

I thought it was kind of ironic that Josh's message tonight was from a Scripture that says we are a "new creation" and how we have to put off the old (bad) things and become new. And while I know Josh was talking about our interior selves (and I do feel that God is making me new inside), it was kind of interesting that my exterior has changed too.

Still, I fully realize that it's the inward changes that matter most. And I do want to grow out of my old ways, like criticizing others or being jealous or just having a bad attitude. I do want to be changed (from the inside out), and I do want to end up looking more like God through and through.

I suppose everything that happened today made me really take a look at this particular "Just Ask" letter.

Dear Jamie,

I've really blown it, and my life is so bad I don't even know who to talk to anymore. I'm sixteen, and my ex-boyfriend introduced me to "recreational" drugs about a year ago. At first I convinced myself that it was no big deal and that I'd never get seriously hooked. But now I'm pretty sure that I'm an addict. My parents are these really normal go-to-church-on-Sunday kind of people and have no idea about my "secret" life. When my grades began slipping, I made up a big excuse, and they even hired a tutor to help me. But now I think I'm pregnant, and I don't know how to tell them. Not only that, my ex-boyfriend just learned that he has HIV, and now I need to get checked too. I feel like just giving up. I mean, what hope is there for someone who's this messed up?

Messed Up and Lost

Dear Lost,

You really do sound like a mess, but I don't think it's hopeless. The first thing you need to do is, come clean with your parents. If they "go to church," they should be willing to forgive you and get you the help you need. Your parents probably love you more than anyone on this earth, and I'm sure they'll never give up on you. Give them a chance to show you who they are and let them help you through this hard time. And you also need to know that God is there for you too. He loves you, no matter how badly you blow it, and He's ready to help you find your way out of this mess. Don't give up. But don't go back to the mistakes you've made either. Get help and get it now!

Just Jamie

Wow, it's amazing that someone could make that many bad choices—and in such a short amount of time too. But then I suppose it could happen to anyone. I hope I'm not wrong about this girl's parents, but if they hired a tutor, they must care about her. I'm really praying that they won't let her down.

Sometimes I wish I could meet some of the kids who write these letters. I'd like to give some of them a great big hug. Even more than that, it makes me REALLY want to reach out to some of the kids I already know. The kinds of kids who look like they're trouble just waiting to happen (like Marissa or Spencer). I mean, Marissa's not really that messed up, but sometimes I get the feeling that she's just one step away from doing something totally stupid. But I could be wrong. I sure hope so. Just the same, I'll keep praying for her and looking for opportunities to reach her.

Sixteen

Tuesday, November 8

I think I was more aware of my makeover than anyone else at school. And that's okay. If anything, I think it's given me more confidence. And in some ways, I was relieved that hardly anyone said anything. I was almost surprised when Marissa finally mentioned it in art class.

"I like your hair," she said.

"Thanks. It was kind of hard getting it cut, but I'm not sorry."

She flipped a long strand of her coal black hair over a shoulder. "Yeah, I think about cutting mine sometimes too, but it's like part of my identity. And now that you cut yours, it makes me even more determined to keep mine just the way it is."

"Good for you," I told her. "Are you going to keep it black too?" Now, I'd been wanting to ask her about this since I've never been able to figure out why she would dye it black on purpose. I mean, I've learned to accept my hair color, though there was a time when I wanted to change it.

"I don't know." She studied my hair then frowned. "Do you have something against black hair?"

I kind of laughed. "No. But I used to want to change my color."

"Why don't you?"

"I tried it once."

"Really? What color?"

"It was in middle school, and I wanted it to be reddish. I'd seen a girl with hair like that, and I thought it looked cool. Natalie helped me do it, and it turned into a total disaster."

She leaned forward with interest. "What happened?"

"It turned kind of a muddy purple color."

"That sounds interesting."

"Mostly it was ugly. I was so embarrassed that I begged my mom to have a professional dye it black again. And then it took years for it to all grow out and look as good as before."

"And then you went and cut it." Marissa frowned like maybe that was a big mistake after all.

I gave my hair a shake, enjoying the feathery feel around my face. "But I really like it this way better."

"I like it too," said Matthew, and I realized that he'd been standing behind us.

"Thanks," I said, feeling embarrassed.

"And I like what you're doing there, Kim." He leaned down and looked at my pencil sketch, pointing to a section of tree that I couldn't get quite right. "You might try shading the trunk in a little around there," he said.

"I think you're right," I told him. "That's exactly what's wrong."

"Any tips for me?" Marissa asked in what sounded like her flirty voice—the one she usually reserves for Cesar.

Matthew squinted as he studied her sketch of what I think was supposed to be a cat unless it was a rabbit. "Start over?" He pretended to duck in case she threw a punch.

"Thanks a lot."

He just shrugged and walked away, but then he said, "Hey, Kim," as he motioned for me to come over to where he was standing in a semisecluded corner.

Curious, I went over to see what he wanted.

"I was thinking about asking you something," he said in a quiet voice, like he didn't want anyone in art to overhear us.

"Ask away."

"Well, remember how I said I want my senior year to be different?"

I nodded.

He exhaled as if whatever he wanted to ask me was going to be difficult. "Well, I wondered if you'd want to go to the Harvest Dance with me next week..."

I considered this. "Sure, why not."

"Cool." He glanced over to where Mr. Fenton was now eyeing us from his office, like he was about to say something. "Guess I better get back to work now."

"Yeah, me too."

I sat back down and tried to act calm, but I now had Marissa staring at me. "What did he want?" she finally demanded.

I just shrugged and continued to work on my sketch, adding the shadows right where Matthew suggested, and he was totally right; they made all the difference.

"Come on," she urges. "What's up?"

Okay, I knew it was no big deal, but somehow I didn't want Marissa to be the first one I told about the dance. I mean she can be such a downer at times. But then I remembered how I'd been praying for her and trying to connect with her. Maybe this would help. "Matthew asked me to the Harvest Dance."

"Oh."

I was somewhat disappointed with her response, but then reminded myself that this was Marissa. What could I expect?

"Well, that's cool," she finally said.

"I think so." I looked at her as she stared down at her drawing. She seemed sad.

"Are you going?" I asked in what probably sounded like a totally patronizing tone.

"Yeah, you bet." She looked up at me with angry-looking eyes. Or maybe it's just the effect of those thick tracks of black eyeliner she circles her entire eyes with.

"You know," I told her. "There are lots of guys who would ask you out if you ever gave anyone the slightest chance. Or if you would ever give up on Cesar. I mean he's not going to date anyone—period. And there's nothing that either you or Natalie can do about it."

"I <u>knew</u> that Natalie liked him too."

Oops! I really didn't mean to let that slip out.

"Oh, I don't know if she likes him like that," I said quickly, trying to recover from my blooper. "It's just that she thinks it's weird that he doesn't date. Like he's this project that she'd like to figure out."

"Yeah, sure." Marissa looked unconvinced.

"But really—" I tried to distract her from Nat—"there are lots of guys who'd take you to the dance."

"Name one."

"How about Jake?"

"How about him?" Her voice was laced with sarcasm now.

"He can be fun."

She rolled her eyes. "Easy for you to say when you've already scored a date with Mr. Hottie over there." She cussed quietly. "I just don't see why Cesar can't bend his rules for once. I can tell he likes me."

"Really?"

She nodded. "Yeah. Back when I first came to school here he couldn't keep his eyes off me." She frowned. "That is, until Chloe moved in on him."

"Oh."

"Well, there are other guys besides Jake, Marissa." I

looked over by the window to where Robert Sanchez was sitting. "How about Robert? He's definitely good looking."

She followed my gaze and actually seemed to consider this.

"And he's Latino," I reminded her, as if she were blind. "Maybe not as handsome as Cesar, but he's definitely got something going on."

"Kind of short though."

"Well, it's not like you have to wear six-inch heels."

She actually laughed now. "Like it's a done deal, right? Like you think he'd really ask me out."

"He might, with some encouragement."

"And that's going to come from where?"

I smiled.

"Yeah, you bet."

"Hey, if you want, I'll go and—"

"No way."

"So you wouldn't go with him?"

"That's just too lame, Kim. I'm not going to have you running over there and begging Robert Sanchez to take me out like I'm some kind of pathetic charity case."

I shrugged. "Well, I just thought I'd offer."

Now she seemed to be considering something. "But maybe…"

"Maybe what?"

"Maybe you could talk to Matthew. He and Robert hang together in art sometimes. Maybe Matthew could sort of sound Robert out about this stupid idea. At least, that might be a little less embarrassing."

"Okay," I agreed. And that's how I got Matthew to talk to Robert, and by the end of class, it was settled that the four of us would go to the dance together. Well, go figure! Who would've guessed?

"You're doing what?" Natalie demands after Marissa spilled <u>my</u> news at the lunch table.

"Going to the Harvest Dance," I said in a quiet voice. "Is that a problem?"

Nat frowns at me. "With Matthew Barclay?"

"Yeah. Is that like okay with you?"

She shrugged.

"And Marissa is going with Robert Sanchez." I hoped to deflect some of the attention from myself.

"And it's going to be a double date." Marissa seemed just a little too smug.

"A <u>double date</u>?" Natalie actually looked slightly hurt now.

"I know," I said suddenly. "Why don't a bunch of us go together? Kind of a group thing, you know." I looked at Cesar now. "You could come too, Cesar. I mean since it wouldn't be a real date."

He nodded. "Yeah, I've done stuff like that in the past. It's kind of a fun way to hang with friends without feeling like I'm compromising anything."

"How about me?" said Jake.

"Of course," I told him.

"Maybe we should rent a limo," suggested Cesar. "You know split up the cost between all of us and then we could arrive at the dance in style."

I grinned. "I like your thinking." Of course, then I remembered something—like I have someone else to consider about this. "But I, uh, I better check with Matthew before I sign us up."

"Well, I'm sure I can talk ol' Roberto into it," said Cesar. "I'll ask him about it in history this afternoon."

So now I'm feeling a little worried. I mean Matthew's the one who asked me to the dance and it should probably be up to him as to how we get there and who we go with. Still, I'm hoping he'll go for this whole group thing. It seems like it'd be a lot less pressure. I just need to think of a way to ask him that doesn't sound too pushy. Speaking of pushy, get a load of this letter.

Dear Jamie,

I'd like to know how you got picked to write this column for the newspaper. I'm a good writer too, and I think I might do a better job of answering some of the questions than you. Especially the ones about relationships, since I've had lots of boyfriends and interesting experiences that have taught me a lot about life and love. Have you ever considered sharing your column with someone else? That way you could take a break sometimes. So who should I talk to about this possibility? Or do you think you could pass my letter along to whoever it is that makes these decisions? Thank you.

Writer Chick

[She actually gave her real name, as well as phone number and address, but I left it off for the purpose of publication.]

> *Dear Writer Chick,*
> *That's very generous of you to offer to help me write this column. And I'll be sure to pass a copy of your letter to the right person. So far I haven't felt the need to share my column with another writer. But I am a little concerned that you think I haven't done an adequate job with it, and I'd be curious to hear feedback from other kids who read Just Ask. Anyone else out there who thinks it's time for me to hang up my keyboard? I realize that it's impossible to answer every letter perfectly (it's not like this is a science), but I try to do my best, and I hope my answers are somewhat helpful. If you're so interested in giving advice, you might want to consider starting a column of your own.*
> *Just Jamie*

Okay, I'm trying not to feel too irked at this girl. But she has a lot of nerve. I showed her letter to my dad, and he's the one who suggested I answer her publicly in the column. Now I'll be curious to see if any other kids speak up. Who knows? Maybe I really flop at this advice stuff. All I have to go on is my friends' comments, and while they don't love or agree with every answer in my column, they do seem to enjoy reading it. Plus the jury is still out on whether Jamie is a guy or a girl. During these discussions, I usually act like I think Jamie is a guy with a strong feminine side. Not gay, but comfortable with girl questions.

However, I did have one close call in regard to the column last week. It was a result of the letter about not being attractive to the opposite sex that was printed. Natalie remembered the conversation we'd had where I said I was going to write Jamie for advice.

"Did you write that letter?" she demanded the next day.

Naturally, I played dumb, like I hadn't even read the column yet. Then after she pestered me enough, I actually had to lie to her. "Yes," I stupidly told her. "I wrote that letter. You happy now?"

"But why did you make up that stuff about sports and say that you'd had a crush on that guy for two years?"

"To cover my tracks. Do you think I wanted anyone to know it was really me?"

She nodded. "That makes sense." She smiled. "That was pretty creative. I'll have to remember that if I ever write a letter to Jamie."

I laughed. "Yeah, sure, what would you write about?"

"Lots of things."

Okay, I felt bad about lying and even confessed to God and told Him I was sorry. I'd tell Nat too, but then she'd want to know why, and I might end up blowing my cover. It's not easy being an anonymous advice columnist.

After this discussion with Nat, I began reading the letters more carefully, wondering if maybe she had already written one and I'd missed it. Some of the letters are handwritten and if I tried hard enough I might be able to guess the author by the handwriting. But a lot of them are sent through e-mail (where their e-mail addresses are stripped away at the newspaper—for anonymity reasons). But I do get curious sometimes. It's weird to think that I might have gotten letters from kids I actually know.

Sometimes I wonder how I would feel if it suddenly became common knowledge that I, Kim Peterson, am really Jamie. I'd be totally embarrassed—as in I might need to change my identity and move to an undisclosed location. Because it's not like you want your friends to know that you're some lame advice columnist—a little Miss Smarty Pants who thinks she knows everything.

But even more than that, I think I'd be sad to have to stop writing for the paper. I actually like it more than I realized I would. But without the anonymity, it would be almost impossible to continue. And as bad as I feel for lying to Natalie last week, I don't see how I could've done it any other way. Even so, I'm asking God to help preserve my anonymity—if He wants me to keep writing this column—and hopefully I won't be in a situation where I have to lie again.

Seventeen

Saturday, November 12

I am so relieved that Matthew agreed to do the group date thing for the Harvest Dance. And he actually liked the limo idea too. Cesar went out of his way to talk to him about it, and now Matthew says that he thinks Cesar is okay too. That's interesting when you consider what a loner Matthew is. But like he said, he wants his senior year to be different.

So Natalie, Marissa, and I headed to the mall today to look for dresses. Nat wasn't too thrilled that Marissa was coming, but she managed to keep it light as we shopped around. And Marissa was surprisingly nice. She even told us about this time that she went shopping with Chloe and Allie and actually shoplifted some thongs.

"You stole something?" Natalie looked stunned.

"Yeah, it wasn't a big deal."

Suddenly I felt concerned. "You're not still into that, are you?" I looked her right in the eyes in hope that I could tell if she was being honest or not. You never know with this girl. It's like she has this whole different set of values than Nat or me.

"Don't worry; I gave up my life of crime a long time ago." She sighed. "But I still miss the thrill sometimes."

"Well, don't go missing it today," Natalie warned her.

"Don't worry. My dad's a cop, and he's made it pretty clear that I'll be in serious trouble if I ever do it again."

"Your dad's a cop?" I asked incredulously.

"Yeah, it's great," Marissa said sarcastically. "I feel so safe."

"I think that's cool," said Nat.

"You would." Marissa rolled her eyes as we went into this hot new store that Natalie swears by. Well, she doesn't actually swear. We'd barely gone through the door when Marissa spotted this shiny black dress and held it up to show us. Of course, she fell totally in love with it. But I wasn't so sure.

I mean, it was cut so low that I thought her belly button might show, among other things. Plus, it had a slit clear to her thigh. But she insisted on trying it on, and I'll have to admit she looked pretty hot. Okay, maybe a little too hot. But she was not to be talked out of it.

"Poor Robert," Natalie said as Marissa took her dress up to the cash register. "He won't know what hit him."

"I doubt he'll be complaining much," I said as I followed Nat around the store looking for dresses. Of course, I didn't mention that Marissa's choice of dress might've been more for Cesar's benefit than Robert's. No need to get Natalie worked up about something like this now.

Besides, I'd already noticed how much Nat was really getting into this group date thing, and I'd be surprised if she wasn't already imagining that she would be the one hanging with Cesar for most of the evening. She'd already mentioned that she planned to dance with him a few times. Oh, well.

As I pawed through the racks and tried on a variety of less-than-cool dresses, Natalie soon found a dress that suited her. I wasn't surprised that she picked out something much less revealing than Marissa's little number. For one thing, Nat's mother has her standards when it comes to Natalie's wardrobe. They used to fight about clothes all the time, but I think Nat has finally began to realize that her mom isn't totally off base. And although Nat still wears T-shirts that show her midriff occasionally, she only does this when her mom's not around to say something.

Nat's dress was the same color as her eyes—kind of a robin's egg blue. It was a shimmering kind of fabric, and the cut was perfect for her height. To be honest, I think Nat will look lots prettier in her dress than Marissa playing sex goddess in hers.

Now the only problem left was me. It soon became clear that nothing in this store really seemed right for me. Whenever I found something close, it ended up being too long or too big or both. It was one of those times when I'd give anything to be about six inches taller.

"Why don't you try that petite shop across the way," suggested the salesgirl. I think she wanted to get rid of us.

So we wandered over to what looked more like an old lady shop to me. Like the kinds of clothes a midget career woman might wear to the office. But Natalie was being a good sport, and she went straight to the counter and asked if they had anything that would work for me.

"We've got a big rack of formal dresses in the back," the lady told us. "Some new ones just came in yesterday."

So, as I was flipping through the hangers and thinking that it was hopeless, Natalie pulled out a dress and held it up. Now it was seriously red—I mean, like fire-engine, stoplight, bleeding-heart, RED. "It's your size," she said as if that meant something.

"I don't think so…" I shook my head as I frowned at the dress.

"Try it," said Marissa. "You might be surprised."

"But it's so—so red."

"It's pretty," said Nat, then she shoved the dress at me and started ushering me to the changing room.

"I'll look around and see if there's anything else out here," called Marissa. "But my vote is for the red."

Okay, I knew that I wouldn't want to be caught dead in this color, but I also knew that I had to try it on in order to shut those two up. Although I must admit it seemed slightly ironic that Nat and Marissa finally agreed on something.

Feeling bright and conspicuous, I stepped out of the dressing room and limply held out my arms, waiting for their reactions.

"Wow," said Marissa. "You look totally hot."

"As in red hot?" I examine my reflection in the mirror on the wall. "As in where-are-my-sunglasses hot?"

"As in that dress is perfect hot," said Natalie. "Look at that neckline and the length and everything. It's like totally made for you."

"But it's so red."

"Yeah?" Nat was wearing her don't-argue-with-me expression now. "And what's wrong with that?"

"Yeah," said Marissa. "What's wrong with that? It looks great."

I looked down at the satiny fabric and sighed. "It just feels kind of sleazy to me. Kind of like something a hooker might wear."

Okay, this only made them laugh.

"Sure, you bet," Natalie says, as if she was the local hooker expert. "You see hookers wearing dresses just like that all the time. You must be thinking of some old fifties flick, Kim."

"Yeah, get real," agreed Marissa. "The last time I saw a hooker she had on shorts and a tank top."

"Don't worry," said Natalie. "No one will ever confuse you for a hooker, Kim. Your face is too sweet and innocent for that kind of stupidity."

I rolled my eyes, then looked back at the very red dress. "But it just doesn't feel like me. Like I don't know if I'd be comfortable—"

Marissa grabbed my hand. "Let's see if you can dance in it."

So we danced a little, and I have to admit the dress felt okay. I liked the way the skirt moved, and it was actually pretty comfortable.

"Come on," urged Nat. "Just get it."

"Yeah," said Marissa. "Lighten up and have some fun for once."

So I gave in and got the stupid dress. And now it's hanging in my closet like this alien from another planet—probably Mars since it's red too. And I'm sure my other clothes are in total shock. I left the tags on though. And I told my mom that I plan to take it back.

"But why?" she insists after I try it on for her. "You look beautiful, Kim. Red is a wonderful color on you. Look how beautiful it is against your skin, and it makes your eyes sparkle like jewels."

I study my reflection in my bedroom mirror, but just can't see it. All I can see was red.

"You just need a little lipstick," she says quickly. "Hold on a minute." Then she heads off to her room.

Okay, now I'm getting worried. Like does my mom actually think I'm going to wear some of her lipstick? Don't get me wrong, my mom is the sweetest woman I know, but her idea of dressing up is putting on pearls and red lipstick. And okay, the red lipstick might work for her, and my dad seems to love it. But I know it'll look totally lame on me. But here she comes, not only with a tube of lipstick but several other things as well. I take in a deep breath and brace myself. At least no one else is around to witness this spectacle.

"Now just relax, Kimmy," she tells me in the kind of soothing voice that she often used when it was time to take some nasty tasting cough syrup. "It's perfectly fine if you don't like this, but just let me have a little mommy fun, okay?"

Then she turns me away from the mirror and proceeds to apply some of her bright red lipstick and then some blush and even some eye shadow. She uses a Kleenex to fiddle with it for a bit, then turns me around to face the mirror.

To my surprise, it's not that bad. I study it for a while, then finally nod. "Yeah, that kind of works, doesn't it?"

Then as I'm standing there, I feel her slipping something cool around my neck. "And while we're at it, let's just try these too," she says. And I can see that it's her pearl necklace.

I study my reflection for a long moment and decide that I actually look astonishingly glamorous. "I like it," I finally tell her, and she stands behind me with this huge smile on her face.

"You look like a movie star," she says happily.

I keep staring at myself. "It's really not bad, is it?"

"You're so beautiful, Kimmy. Can't you see it?"

I smile now. "Yeah, I guess I sort of can."

Then she hugs me, and I'm thinking maybe my mom's fashion sense isn't totally outdated after all. I tell her thanks, then sort of examine myself from a couple of angles to see if it really looks okay. Like it's not just some sort of optical illusion.

"I mean, I would never want to wear this much makeup on a daily basis," I tell her. "But for the dance...well, maybe it would be okay."

She nods. "It'll be just fine, sweetheart."

So it's settled. I'm keeping the dress, borrowing my mom's makeup and pearls, and she's even going to let me wear her pearl earrings, which look like little droplets. And she wants to go shoe shopping with me after church tomorrow. Of course, I doubt that she'll be much help in the shoe department, since her footwear of choice leans more toward comfortable leather with soft rubber soles. But it'll be fun anyway. And I can tell she's really looking forward to it.

As I took some time to answer some "Just Ask" letters later this afternoon, there was one in particular that really stood out. And not for the first time, it made me thankful for my parents.

Dear Jamie,

My parents got divorced when I was little, and my mom took off and left my brother and me to live with our dad. For the most part, things have gone okay, but then my dad got married last year and I feel just like Cinderella now. My stepmom likes my brother just fine,

but it's like she can't stand me. I mean, she acts all
sweet and nice when my dad's around. But as soon as
he's gone, she starts picking on me about my clothes,
and she wants me to do all the housework, and nothing
I do is ever good enough for her. I am so sick of her
that I feel like asking my grandma if I can live with her.
But then I'd have to move away and leave my friends
and school and stuff. What should I do?

    Can't Take Any More

Okay, how do you answer something like that? Now
I don't have any idea how old this girl is, like she could
be thirteen and have at least five more years of living at
home with this horrible woman. Or maybe she's about
to graduate and can get out of there soon. But my guess
is she must at least have a couple of years before she
can escape. So what do I tell her? This one is definitely
going to take some divine help. So I pray first and
answer later.

Dear CTA,

    *It sounds like you're in a really tough spot. And
sometimes there just aren't any easy answers. So I'm
going to tell you what I would do if I were you. First of
all, I'd ask God to help me because it sounds as if
you're up against something that's going to take a lot of
time and patience to sort out—and you might need help.
Next I would talk to my dad. But I'd try to do this very
carefully. You don't want to make him feel like it's his*

*fault, like he married a wicked witch and you're paying
the price. And then I think the three of you (maybe your
brother too) should all sit down and talk about how
you're feeling and why. If that can't happen without
people getting angry or hurt, you may need to consider
some form of family counseling. But the fact is, if your
dad really loves this woman, she will probably be
around for a long time. And the sooner you figure out a
way to get along with her, the happier you will all be. In
the meantime, hang in there!*
    Just Jamie

I'm not sure that my answer is really going to help
this poor girl, but it might make her feel better to know
that someone's listening and that someone cares. I don't
know what I'd do if I lived in a cruddy situation like that.
Thankfully, I don't.

As I walked past the family room this evening (on
my way out to youth group), I saw my mom and dad
sitting all relaxed in their matching recliners with their feet
up, sharing a bowl of popcorn on the table between
them, and just laughing over some silly old movie. And
okay, they might be frumpy and a little old-fashioned,
but I am so totally thankful for them.

Eighteen

Thursday, November 17

Everyone is all jazzed about the dance this weekend. And I feel a little surprised that I'm excited too. My shoe shopping with Mom was relatively painless, since she wore out early on and then happily agreed to get me these amazing black shoes with the tallest heels I've ever worn. It's like they make me almost normal height. Of course, I didn't admit to my mom that I wasn't sure how long my feet would survive that kind of torture. But hey, it's probably worth it. "Just don't break anything," she warned as I practiced walking around the house in them later that day.

I didn't want to be pushy, but I was curious about what Matthew planned to wear to the dance. It's not like guys go out and rent tuxes or anything.

"I'm going to surprise you," he told me during art

earlier this week. "But I think you'll like it."

And since Matthew has an artist's flair, I'm pretty sure I won't be disappointed. But I told him a little about my dress, just in case he was planning on wearing something that would totally clash. I also wanted him to be warned as to the color. Artists can be very sensitive to color. But he was totally cool about it. "Red sounds great," he told me. "And it works with what I plan to wear too."

So we're set. Naturally, Nat had been hanging around Cesar this week, like she thought she could get him into thinking he's going to be her date. But then he pulled a fast one.

"I've invited someone else to join us for the Harvest Dance," he announced at lunch today. "I thought it might be nice to even out the girls and the guys."

"You asked a date?" demanded Marissa.

"No, not a date. Just a girl who wouldn't have gone otherwise. And she can hang with me and Jake and Natalie."

"Who is it?" asked Nat. And I could see the troubled look in her eyes. Like some hot chick was going to ace her out of being with Cesar.

"Marty Ruez," he told her.

"Why her again?" Marissa asked as she narrowed her eyes at Cesar. "Is it like you think she's going to protect you or something?"

"Nah." Jake winked at his buddy. "Cesar's just got it

bad for Marty. It's his little secret."

"Yeah, whatever," said Cesar. "I happen to think she's nice. And she's fun, and she was happy to join us. Is it a problem?"

"Not at all," I told him. "The more the merrier."

"Yeah," agreed Nat. And I could tell she was relieved (since Marty isn't like the most attractive girl in the school). "No problem."

But now, as I'm sitting here trying to come up with an answer to this "Just Ask" letter, I'm thinking about Marty. In fact, I'm wondering if it's possible that she wrote this letter. If not, maybe she could've.

Dear Jamie,

I hate my life. And I hate my big fat body. I can never lose any weight. And it doesn't help that everyone picks on me because of my weight. I'm not chubby or pleasantly plump either, I'm just plain fat—the kind of fat that strangers make fun of. Sometimes I think I can't take it for one more day. I hate going to school. I hate walking down the hall or finding a desk in the classroom. I hate going to lunch or being seen eating anything. I just don't see how life can be worth living like this. Why do people hate you because you're fat? Why do they think it's okay to treat you like crud because you're overweight? Don't they know you're already suffering enough? It's just not fair!

Fat 'n' Miserable

Dear FnM,

    Wow, you do sound miserable. And while it's wrong for people to tease you about your weight, there's nothing you can do about that. But if you're really miserable, then maybe you can use that frustrated energy to do something. You say you "never lose weight," but I have to wonder what you've tried. I mean, do you exercise daily and cut back on carbs? Because the way I see it, you're the only one who can change anything about yourself. And if you hate your body and your life, then you should do something! And maybe you'll feel better when you realize that you have some control over your weight—because only you can control what you eat and how much you exercise. You may also need some outside help, like joining a fitness club or a weight loss clinic or just getting a really good diet book and following it. But I really believe if you want this enough, you can do it. And by the way, if I were you, I'd ask God to help me get and stay on track. You may also need to talk to your doctor first. But why not decide to take control—and why not do it today?

    Just Jamie

I had to throw in the last doctor part because of something my dad warned me about. He said that I couldn't say anything that could be perceived as "medical advice" without also telling the person to consult her physician first. Although I can't imagine what doctor wouldn't agree that anyone who wants to lose weight should eat less and exercise more. But hey, I'd rather be safe than sorry.

Still, I'm thinking about Marty Ruez and kids who are heavy. But I don't think she was the one who wrote that letter since she's not horribly obese, just fairly overweight. And she doesn't seem that miserable to me either. I mean, she's a Christian, she goes to youth group, and she's good friends with Cesar. So really, she's probably not that unhappy.

But there is a girl at our school who's seriously fat. I'm guessing she's three hundred pounds or more, although I have no idea. I hardly ever see her, but when I do, it's like you can't miss her. I don't even know her name, but I feel sorry for her. She's always got her head down, and you can tell that she's totally miserable.

I guess I've wondered why she doesn't do anything about it. But then I really don't know how she feels or what her life is like. And now I'm feeling bad that I don't even know her name. I guess I better do something about that.

Sunday, November 20

It's the day after the Harvest Dance. Where do I begin? I have to say that everything started out pretty cool. Then it got a little freaky. But finally it turned out okay, I think. Let me explain.

First of all, it was fun getting ready. Natalie decided to get dressed at my house since her mom had to hire a sitter to watch Krissy and Micah, and Nat didn't want to be around when she arrived. So she came over around five, and then we took our time and had fun doing the whole hair and makeup routine.

And I think my parents (especially my mom) really enjoyed the whole show. And naturally, my mom took lots of pictures, and my dad even broke out the video camera. Nat and I strutted our stuff and hammed it up for him while he taped us. So all in all, I think the parents were pleased.

The plan was for the limo to work its way across town to pick everyone up. Our stop was about midway, and by the time it reached my house, Marissa, Robert, Jake, and Matthew were already inside. Nat and I were ready to hop in and go, but my parents, armed with cameras, insisted that we all have our pictures taken. Of course, this also gave them a chance to meet Matthew, which come to think of it, might have been their ulterior motive all along.

After our Kodak moment, we all piled into the limo, and I got the impression that Marissa had been enjoying being the only girl, and I'm sure that those three guys appreciated her rather revealing dress. Even so, they seemed happy to have Nat and me join their lively little group.

"You look great," Matthew said as he helped me into the stretch limo.

"You look pretty hot yourself." I checked out what

appeared to be a dinner jacket from the sixties. "Where did you get that?"

He laughed. "My mom is the costume designer for the community theater. She let me go through her stuff."

"Wow, this is awesome." I checked out the long leather seats along the inside of this incredibly luxurious car.

"Totally cool," Nat said as she sat between Robert and Jake.

"They even have a bar." Marissa held up a plastic cup of what I assumed was sparkling cider since I could see a couple of opened bottles in the bar area. "Want some?"

"Sure," I told her. "That sounds great."

"Me too," said Nat.

Jake raised his hand. "You guys might want to—"

"I'll take care of everything." Marissa quickly reached for the bottle and poured out two glasses.

Robert took the glasses and handed them to us. Then he and Marissa and Matthew lifted their glasses in a toast.

"To an awesome evening," Marissa said happily.

Well, as soon as I took a sip I could tell that it didn't taste quite right. "What is this?" I asked Marissa, but she just giggled.

"Is there something in this drink?" Natalie sniffed the contents of her cup.

I took another cautious sip, then decided that maybe

I imagined it. But that's when I noticed that Jake didn't have a cup. Not only that, but he had a funny look on his face.

"What's up?" I asked him.

"Nothing," Marissa said with a sly expression. "Drink up, girls."

I turned to Matthew now. "Is this spiked?"

He kind of smiled. "Is that a problem?"

I frowned. "Yeah. That's a problem."

"I tried to warn you," said Jake. "But as usual, no one listens to me. She pulled this same little stunt on me too."

"You're just a wet blanket," said Marissa. "Come on, you guys, one little drink isn't going to hurt anyone."

"I can't believe you did this." Natalie held her cup away from her at arm's length, as if it were poison.

"Yeah," I agreed. "You should've told us."

"Lighten up," said Marissa. "It's just a little vodka. I thought it would be fun."

I glanced up to the driver in front. "You're going to get us all into serious trouble. What if the driver—?"

"Don't worry about him," said Marissa. "He doesn't even speak English."

"But what about—?"

"Hey, I'm not forcing you to drink it," she said defensively. "If you don't want it, don't drink it."

"I don't want it." I handed the cup back to her.

"No problem." She just poured the contents of my cup into her own and took another sip.

"Me neither," said Nat.

"I'll take that for you," Robert said, imitating Marissa's move.

I glanced over at Matthew now. His cup was already empty.

"Does it bother you if I drink?" he asked.

I wasn't sure how to answer but decided to just be honest. "Yeah. It actually does."

"Then I won't." He set his cup aside and smiled at me.

Now I turned and glared at Marissa. "I don't see why you had to do this tonight. We could have fun without alcohol."

She just shrugged. "Don't come unglued, Kim. It's no big deal."

Just then we were stopping at another house, and Cesar joined us. He looked happy and handsome in his khaki pants and dark jacket.

"Everything okay?" he asked as he sat next to Marissa.

I shrugged. "Ask Marissa."

But she just laughed. "Want a drink, Cesar?"

He glanced at the sparkling cider bottles at her elbow. "Sounds good."

"Wait a minute," I said quickly. "You should know what's really in that so-called sparkling cider."

"Yeah." Nat moved over to the other side of Cesar. "Marissa spiked it with vodka."

"And everyone in here has had some," Marissa said

as she smugly held a cup out to Cesar.

"Thanks, but no thanks." Cesar folded his arms across his chest.

"Whatever." Then she split the contents of that cup between her and Robert.

"And I don't think you guys should be drinking either," said Cesar.

But now we were stopping at another house and soon Marty was joining us. Marissa didn't even offer Marty a drink. But before Marty could feel slighted by this, Cesar explained.

"Marissa spiked the sparkling cider," he told her. "She gave some to Jake and Nat and Kim without them knowing what was up."

"That's real intelligent," said Marty.

"Yeah, that's what I'm thinking," I agreed.

"Well, let's not let these idiots ruin it for everyone," said Jake. "We can still have fun tonight."

"I should've warned you that we were riding in the kiddie car, Robert." Marissa poured herself another drink.

"Haven't you had enough?" asked Cesar.

"What's it to you?" Marissa leaned over far enough for him to see clear to her belly button.

I watched Cesar to see how he would handle this. But he just turned and looked away. I could tell he was uncomfortable, and I felt seriously irked at Marissa for spoiling things like this. But really, what could you do? What would Just Jamie say? To distract myself, I looked out the window and imagined the letter I would write.

Dear Jamie,

I was going to a dance with friends tonight when a couple of them started drinking sparkling cider spiked with vodka. We were all stuck in this limo together, and I didn't know what to do. What would you do in this situation?

Stuck with Stupid

Dear Stuck,

Well, I'm not a legal expert, but I think that everyone in the limo could've gotten into trouble if you'd been caught. Maybe you should've asked the limo driver to pull over and put the offenders out on the street so the rest of you could travel to the dance in peace.

Just Jamie

Of course, by the time I arrived at this solution, we were at the restaurant. But Cesar was the first one to get out, and he took the two bottles of "sparkling cider," then tossed them in the trash can on the sidewalk.

"What're you doing?" demanded Marissa as she chased after him.

"Keeping us all out of trouble."

"That wasn't yours to throw away," she said.

"This evening isn't <u>yours</u> to throw away." He turned back to the limo to help Marty out.

Matthew helped me out of the limo, and Jake helped Nat. I could tell she was slightly disappointed that she was getting paired with Jake, but knowing Nat, I figured she'd be a good sport. We'd all agreed on a moderately priced restaurant, and Cesar had made reservations. But when we got inside we realized that we were being split into two groups. As it turned out, Matthew and I got stuck with the boozers, and the rest were seated across the room.

"Are you mad at me?" Matthew asked me quietly.

I forced a smile that probably wasn't very believable. "Not you." Then I glanced across the table at Marissa and Robert. Okay, I wasn't just mad at them; I was borderline furious. Why did they want to ruin everything for everyone?

Matthew nodded. "Don't let it get to you."

"Yeah," said Marissa. "You should lighten up, Kim. Have some fun for a change." Then she turned to Robert and giggled like she'd just said something extremely funny. Whatever.

Dinner went relatively smoothly. Matthew and I actually had a decent conversation, and I even began to relax a little when it seemed clear that Marissa and Robert weren't going to act like complete morons. Although I wished Marissa had eaten more than a few bites of her salad. The thought of her with all that vodka and not much food in her stomach was not encouraging.

I did think it was interesting that Robert and Marissa seemed to be getting along so well. It seemed that every time I looked across the table at them, they had their heads together and were laughing over some private joke. Which was fine with me since I really didn't want to talk to them much anyway.

But finally I noticed something that set off my alarms again. "What is that?" I asked Marissa as she handed what looked like a small bottle back to Robert.

She gave me this cheesy grin. "None of your business."

"I'm serious. What are you guys hiding over there?"

"Just let it go, Kim," warned Matthew.

"Why? What is it?"

He kind of shrugged, but I could tell he knew.

"They're drinking again, aren't they?" I looked at glasses of what I'd assumed was straight iced tea and sighed.

"Wha's the big deal?" demanded Marissa, and I could tell her speech was getting slurred.

I turned to Matthew. "Excuse me, please."

He just nodded as I left the table and went to the ladies' room. Okay, maybe I was overreacting or being a spoilsport or whatever, but Marissa and Robert were making me really mad. Not only that, but my feet were starting to hurt. Why on earth did I want to go to this stupid dance tonight?

I went into the bathroom and into a stall where I just stood there fighting back tears of anger. But I wasn't sure what I was most angry about. I mean, I was angry at the boozers, but I was also angry at myself for getting so upset by this. Why couldn't I just chill? Why do I always make a big deal about things?

Finally, I realized that the only thing I could really do at that moment was to pray. So, standing there in the stall of the bathroom, I asked God to take what was looking like a lousy evening and make it into something worthwhile. I asked God to change my attitude of anger and judgment against Marissa and Robert into one of grace and love.

Now I wasn't sure what that would mean exactly. It's not like I thought they should be riding with us and boozing it up. But at least I wasn't feeling so freaked now. I stopped by the other table on my way back from the ladies' room and clued Cesar (the sort of unspoken leader) about what was going on at my table.

Fortunately, he didn't seem too surprised. "We'll figure something out," he said in that assuring way of his.

As it turned out, we didn't have to. By the time we finished dinner and went back out to wait for the limo to pick us up, Marissa was acting weird. I mean, it was obvious she was drunk, but it looked like her eyes weren't even focusing as she stood leaning against Robert and blabbering rather incoherently. Although the rest of the group seemed to be looking the other way.

"Are you okay?" I asked.

"I'm jus' okeydokey," she said with a spaced-out smile.

"You don't look too good," I said.

"Just ignore her," Matthew suggested as he tugged me away.

"There's the limo." Jake pointed down the street.

But before I turned to look, I saw Marissa swaying. "Hang on to her, Robert," I yelled, but too late. The next thing we knew, Marissa was literally facedown on the sidewalk. Robert and I knelt down to help pick her up. And just as we got her to her feet, she leaned over to Robert and hurled all over his dark jacket. And man, was that a stink!

Nat and Jake just started laughing. But I actually felt sorry for Marissa, and Robert too, for that matter. Still, I wasn't sure what to do. But in that same moment, a taxi came by and Cesar flagged it down. And before they knew what hit them, Cesar and Jake had loaded the two boozers into the cab and slammed the door behind them.

"Do you think they'll be okay?" I asked, still feeling slightly stunned by the quick turn of events.

"I told the driver that he should probably take them home," said Cesar.

"Man, I feel sorry for the guy who has to clean that cab up," said Jake. "Whew, they were a mess!"

Then we all climbed into the limo, went to the dance, and actually had a really fun time. And we never saw Robert or Marissa for the rest of the night. And although I was relieved they were gone, I felt sorry for them. I'm sure that wasn't the way they'd planned for the evening to go.

Nineteen

Tuesday, November 22

Funny how both Marissa and Robert kept an extremely low profile in school yesterday. Today they acted a little more normal, but sheepish still. At least, that's how I would describe it. And Marissa's mouth wasn't doing its usual lunchtime commentary thing either. In a way, it was kind of refreshing. The first actual conversation I had with her was in art today.

"Sorry that I messed things up for the Harvest Dance," she kind of mumbled about midway through class.

"Huh?" I looked up from my drawing in surprise.

She made a face and rolled her eyes. "Look, I just said I'm sorry. Okay?"

"Sure," I told her. "I was actually feeling sorry for you that night. You were pretty sick."

"Tell me about it."

"Did the cab driver take you home?"

"Yeah." She shook her head. "Whose brilliant idea was that anyway?"

I kind of shrugged, not wanting to pin all the blame on Cesar since I thought it was the best thing to do at the time too. "Did you get in trouble?"

"Fortunately, my dad wasn't home. And even though my mom was seriously irked, she kind of covered for me."

"The dance was really fun," I said as I switched pencils.

"I don't want to hear about it."

"Fine."

Now Matthew came up and put his hand on my shoulder. "How's it going?"

I smiled up at him. "Okay."

"Nice work," he said as he studied my sketch.

"Thanks."

Then he went back to his own picture.

"What's up with you guys?" Marissa said as soon as he was out of earshot.

"I don't know."

"Come on."

Now seriously, I don't really know. I mean, we had a great time at the dance. And I really like him, and I think he likes me. And when he walked me to my door from the limo that night, he even kissed me. Just once. But I have to admit it was a good kiss, and I wouldn't have minded if he'd done it again. And since Nat had already been dropped off, Matthew and I had been the last ones in the limo, so it's not as if anyone was sitting around watching us. But then he just politely said good night. And that was it. We talked like normal on Monday and again today. But that's really about it.

"We had fun at the dance," I told Marissa. "Matthew's a great guy, and I like him. But seriously, I don't know where it's going."

She glanced over her shoulder to where Matthew seemed completely immersed in his work. "Yeah, whatever. Leave it to you to mess up your chance with a pretty decent guy."

I frowned. "What's that supposed to mean?"

She just shrugged. "Figure it out yourself, smarty."

"Yeah. Whatever." Then I focused my attention back onto my sketch and tried not to let her words get to me. But it was useless.

And that's why I decided to answer one of these what-do-I-do-about-this-guy kind of letters tonight. Honestly, the "Just Ask" column gets more letters like this than anything else. And for the most part, I ignore them. I mean, the answers seem obvious—like duh, what do you think you should do?

But it's as though these girls need some kind of confirmation, like Jamie is going to write something like, "Of course, this guy must really like you. He's probably deeply in love with you but just afraid to show it. Don't worry; I'm sure that you'll get married someday and have lots of lovely children." Yeah, right. The true answer would probably go more like, "Sorry, it sounds like this dude could care less about going out with you. Why don't you just forget about him and get a life." But naturally, I don't write that. It would be too heartless and cruel.

Still, I decided that I should attempt a response to one of these tonight.

Dear Jamie,

There's this guy who I've known for years. And I really like him, and I think he likes me too. And we have these great conversations and stuff. But lately he's been acting interested in this other girl. And he asked me if I thought he should ask her out. I said "I don't know." But I really wanted to tell him that she's the meanest stuck-up witch in the school and that he should go out with me instead. But I didn't. What should I do now?

Unlucky in Love

Dear Unlucky,

That must be hard for you. But here's the good news—since you're good friends with this guy, I'm guessing your relationship with him will last longer than with the "stuck-up witch." So maybe you should just hang in there and be his friend, especially if his heart gets broken by this other girl (that is, if she's really as mean as you think she is). And maybe in time, if he

really likes you as much as you think, maybe he'll
decide he wants to ask you out. And if not, at least you
still have a good friend. Nothing wrong with that.
    Just Jamie

So now I'm thinking maybe that's how I should look
at this thing with Matthew. Okay, maybe he doesn't want
to take me out again. I wouldn't be surprised after the
tizzy fit I threw over the boozers in the limo and at
dinner. I'm sure I was a big wet blanket. But then, what
do you do in that situation? And despite everything, it
turned out okay. Well, fairly okay.

Robert and Marissa didn't have much of a night. But
I'm just thinking—hey, whatever…if Matthew wants to
go out, it's cool. If not, it's cool. And the reason I feel this
laid-back about it is because I've decided to give the
whole thing to God to work out.

I think the reason I have this kind of confidence has
to do with my prayer in the bathroom at the restaurant.
It's like if God could sort that silly mess out, I'm sure He
can sort all kinds of things out. I just need to learn to
trust Him.

Now I need to go down and clean up the kitchen.
Not my favorite household chore, but I promised my
dad that I'd do it, and it's getting late. And my mom's
been feeling pretty crummy lately. I guess she's still going
through "the change" (as she calls it), although most
normal people just call it menopause.

But my mom's kind of funny about things like that.

Like having these code words she thinks no one can decipher when she's describing some "feminine condition." Like why not just call cramps "cramps" or a tampon a "tampon" or a period a "period"—period? What's the big deal? But I guess it had to do with the era she grew up in or her mom or something. Anyway, I hope her menopause ends soon. I can tell it's a drag.

Friday, November 25

Yesterday was Thanksgiving, but we didn't really do anything much because my mom was still feeling lousy with her change-of-life condition. My dad baked a turkey breast and made dressing out of a box, but we mostly just sat around and watched TV. Pretty boring. And then Mom went to bed because she was feeling so bad. Naturally, this worried my dad. He was so worried, in fact, that he actually called her doctor first thing this morning, made an appointment for this afternoon, then made me promise to drive her.

Well, I was feeling kind of irked since it was my day off and there were things I'd rather be doing than sitting in some stuffy doctor's office waiting for my mom. But then I realized how selfish I was being and gave in. And I guess I'm glad that I did. Well, a sad kind of glad.

My mom absolutely hates going to the doctor and avoids it whenever possible. So she wasn't too happy to have me dragging her in today. But it was good that we went, because after some preliminary tests, her doctor now wants her to have more tests at the hospital. These have already been scheduled for next week.

Now Mom's acting like this is just going to be a huge inconvenience to everyone, but Dad and I are thinking it's probably a good thing. If there's a chance that something is wrong, it's better to find out and get it fixed, right? That's what I think. But at the same time, I have to admit that I'm a little worried. I mean, what if it's something big?

"It's just the change," Mom reassured me as I drove her Buick toward home. "It's harder on some women than others, and it runs in families. My mother was the same way at this age and so was my grandma."

At first I started to assume that meant I'd be like that too, then, of course, I remembered my birth roots are from an entirely different gene pool. "That's too bad it makes you feel so cruddy," I told her as I turned down our street. "But maybe these tests will reveal something that's treatable, and your doctor can give you something to make you feel better."

She sighed and leaned back into her seat. "Maybe so."

When I reached the stop sign, I glanced over and was surprised at how pale her face looked and that her eyes were shut. And I don't know why, but I got this chill of fear running through me. It's like she looked so weak and vulnerable. In that split second, I almost gasped.

"Mom?" I said suddenly.

Her eyes popped open, and she turned to look at me. "What's wrong?"

"Are you—are you okay?"

Then she smiled. "Of course, sweetheart. I'm perfectly fine. I'm just a little tired, that's all."

Okay, now that we were home and I'd made her some tomato soup and a cup of her favorite tea, then insisted that she go have a rest, I'm feeling better. I mean, she's my mom and one of the sweetest ladies I know (everyone says so). There's no way someone like my mom could be seriously ill.

Even so, I'm praying for her and asking God to get her past this menopause thing and back to her old self. Because I can tell she's feeling discouraged. And that is so unlike my mom.

To take my mind off my mom, I spend some time answering "Just Ask" letters. And one of them is pretty crazy.

Dear Jamie,

The thing is, my girlfriend is a vegan, and I since I really like her, I became one too. But the problem is, I've been cheating on her lately. I've been eating meat. It's like I can't help myself when I'm not around her. Not only that, but my mom is worried that my teeth are all going to fall out. Should I tell my girlfriend I've been cheating, or should I just keep on pretending to be a vegan when I'm with her? Although I'm afraid she smelled chicken McNuggets on my breath last weekend.

Fakin' Vegan

Dear Fakin',

You might as well fess up to this vegan chick. I mean, the truth always comes out in the end. And if she can't handle dating a meat-eating guy, there's nothing you can do about it. And I'm sure there are lots of nice meat-eating girls out there who will accept you for who you are.

Just Jamie

Wednesday, November 30

My mom goes to the hospital for tests tomorrow. Of course, she keeps telling us that it's no big deal, just routine, blah-blah-blah. But I can tell that Dad's not so sure. The way he's running around and catering to her every whim tells me he's actually quite worried. Of course, he won't admit this. But he's arranged to have the day off and will stay with her in the hospital until the tests are finished.

I offered to ditch school to be with them today, but they told me to forget it. Now, if I wasn't a straight A student, I could understand their concern. But if there's anyone who would not be affected by missing a day or two of classes, it's me.

"I'd feel better knowing you were in school, sweetheart," my mom assured me last night. "There's no need for all of us to disrupt our normal schedule for a few silly tests." So wanting to put her at ease, I decided not to argue. Just the same, I still think they should've let me skip school, just to show that they respected me as a valuable family member and honors student and generally mature person.

On the other hand, I didn't mind going to school so much either. Especially since things with Matthew have suddenly heated up. I have to admit that I felt pretty bad after Thanksgiving weekend. I mean, I actually thought he might've called me or something. But he didn't. Not even once.

Then on Monday, he told me how his parents made him go with them to visit his grandparents, who live in the next state, and how everyone got into this big old fight, but they stayed the whole weekend anyway. I had to feel sorry for him since it all sounded pretty pitiful and lame to me.

That same day he asked me to have lunch with him. Off campus. Now our school has an open-campus policy, but I don't usually leave, because I don't like to risk being late for my next class. Right, it's the type-A thing. However, I decided to risk it for Matthew. How could I say no?

He wanted to go to this little deli a few blocks from school, and since it happened to be sunny (when we left), we decided it would be quicker to just walk. And we had the best lunch—very romantic—and totally lost track of time. By the time we realized it was late and headed back to school, it was raining. Pouring down raining. Cats and dogs raining (which comes from around twelfth century England when pets would sleep in the thatched roof for warmth but come tumbling down when it rained too hard—literally raining cats and dogs).

Anyway, by the time I got to English lit, I was soaking wet, and Mrs. Langford looked at me like I was a juvenile delinquent or degenerate or something pretty disgusting. I apologized for being late and, without going into too much detail, quickly explained (honestly) how I'd been caught in this deluge. And I really don't see why she needed to be concerned, since I doubt I've ever been late for her class before. Just the same, I better not let that happen again.

So when Matthew asked me to have lunch with him today, I had to tell him, "Sure, but we have to stay on campus." So we did. And after we finished lunch and made a graceful exit from our friends' table, Matthew took me to the journalism room (where he works for the yearbook) and showed me some of the photo layouts he'd been working on recently.

"You're so multitalented." I sat and watched as he flipped through the computer program that stores his yearbook layouts.

After a few minutes, he placed his hand on my shoulder, then leaned down over me, putting his face close to mine. And honestly I felt this electrical sensation running up and down my back. Then he kissed me on the neck, and it was totally awesome. I've never felt like that before. And the next thing I knew we were really kissing. Kim Peterson and Matthew Barclay doing some serious mouth-to-mouth right here in the journalism room.

Of course, I nearly jumped out of my skin when I heard someone loudly clearing his throat—the kind of sound meant to announce that someone's just entered the room.

"Hey, Mr. Wong." Matthew casually stood up straight and pushed back the hair that had fallen across his forehead.

"Did I interrupt anything?" Mr. Wong adjusted his glasses but appeared fully aware, if not somewhat amused, by the scene he'd just walked in on.

"Just showing Kim some of my work."

"I'll say."

"I better go," I said quickly. "Thanks for showing me everything, Matthew. See you."

"Later."

Then I zipped right out of there with, I'm sure, blazing cheeks as I hurried on over to the English wing— early for class this time. It took me a couple of minutes to catch my breath, but I pretended to be reading as kids started to trickle into class.

"You and Matthew sure took off in hurry at lunch today," Natalie said as we drove home later that day.

"He wanted to show me something."

"Yeah, I'll bet." Then she started giggling, and I had to tell her about being discovered in the journalism room by Mr. Wong. Of course, this made Nat laugh even harder, but suddenly she stopped and became completely serious.

"But aren't you concerned?" she asked.

"About what?"

"You know, that Matthew's not saved."

I sighed now. I should've seen this coming. Nat's got this big thing about not dating anyone who's "not saved." It's like they're infected with some contagious spiritual disease, and if you go out with them, you'll be infected too. I didn't say anything.

"I mean, he might drag you down, Kim."

"Drag me down?"

"Yeah. His convictions and values probably aren't the same as yours."

"I don't know about that…"

"I just don't think you should get that serious with him."

"I guess that's up to me, Nat, isn't it?"

Now she didn't say anything, and I suspected I'd offended her. "Okay, this is how I see it," I told her. "Not that long ago, I didn't consider myself a Christian. Right?"

"Yeah."

"But that has changed."

"Yeah."

"Well, maybe Matthew's going to change too."

"But you don't know that for sure."

"And you don't know that he's not."

Okay, that seemed to quiet her down. And it was time to change the subject. "I'm heading over to the hospital after I drop you off," I said as we waited at the stoplight.

"How's your mom doing?"

"When I talked to Dad after lunch, she was still knocked out from whatever they gave her while they did their tests. And he thinks they may keep her overnight."

"Just to do tests?"

"I guess so."

"Well, tell her I'm praying for her."

"Thanks."

And I was praying for her too. After dropping Nat off, I prayed out loud even as I drove over to the hospital. "Please, God, make everything okay. Please, show the doctors what's wrong and how to fix it so that Mom can come home and start feeling better than ever!"

But when I find my dad at the hospital, he doesn't seem to know much more than when I talked to him earlier. Even so, he seems concerned.

"They're going to keep her overnight," he tells me.

"Can I see her?"

He smiles. "Of course. That should cheer her up."

"Cheer her up?"

"Well, she's not very excited about spending a night in the hospital." He leads me to her room.

"I don't see why she has to. Maybe the hospital's just trying to make money."

He laughs. "Yeah, that's probably it."

Now we're going into the room, and I feel surprised to see her in the hospital bed with her eyes closed, looking like that same pale and vulnerable woman I remember from our ride home from the doctor last week.

"Is she asleep?" I whisper to my dad.

Then her eyes flutter open, and she smiles and suddenly looks like my mom again. Okay, she's a pale and tired-looking version of my mom, but her blue eyes look clear and bright and happy to see us. "Come in, come in," she says, and we go over to stand by her.

"I'm sorry they're making you spend the night," I say as she reaches for my hand. "That's got to be a drag."

She nods. "But I suppose it's better than getting up at five in the morning and coming in."

"Kim thinks the hospital is just trying to get rich off of you," says Dad.

Mom smiles. "Maybe so." Then she squeezes my hand. "How was your day today, sweetheart?"

I kind of shrug. I haven't really told either of them much about Matthew. I mean, there hasn't been much to tell. Well, until this week. And although I don't want to divulge too much, I figure I owe a little something to Mom (especially seeing her looking so helpless right now).

"Matthew really seems to like me."

She smiles. "He seems like a nice boy."

I tell them about his Thanksgiving weekend and the family feud, and they think that's pretty funny. So then I tell them about going to lunch with him on Monday and getting soaked by the rain. Of course, I don't mention anything about being late to English. Or about being caught kissing today. I mean, you can only tell your parents so much.

But I can tell that Mom's getting tired. "Maybe I should let you rest."

She nods. "And I'm sure you must have homework or some writing for the column or something."

So I kiss her on the cheek. "Hope you can get some good rest." I walk toward the door.

"I'll be home later," calls my dad.

And then I head for home and tell myself that everything's going to be fine. But just to be sure, I pray some more.

Twenty

Thursday, December 1

This day starts out so perfect. I get up early and actually do my morning devotions (it's so hard to do them every day, but I always feel better when I do). And I pray for my mom that the tests will go okay and that the doctors will figure out how to make her feel better.

Then I go to school and ace my history test, and I'm feeling really good. At lunchtime, Matthew asks me to go to a play with him on Friday. And well, it's like I'm just really on top of it. Like nothing can go wrong for me.

And then everything changes.

Last night before I went to bed, I made Dad promise to call me as soon as he found out anything about Mom's tests. And I've been checking my cell all day—but nothing. Still, maybe no news is good news. Maybe they've already gone home by now, and everything is back to normal or better. But then I check messages at around two o'clock, and I see that my dad's called.

"Your mom's tests are done," he says in a voice that doesn't sound quite like him. "Come on over to the hospital, and we can talk."

Okay, now that worries me. It's not like he's saying her tests are done and everything is just fine, but come on over and we can talk. What's up with that? So I go straight to the office and explain. And of course, Mrs. Stannifer (a friend of my mom's) immediately excuses me and tells me to go.

"Let me know how she's doing," she calls as I hurry out.

I try not to race to the hospital. And I tell myself that I might be overreacting. It's entirely possible that my dad just wants to tell me the good news in person—for a nice surprise. But somehow I don't quite believe this. Even so, I am praying hard and with what feels like real faith, and I am asking God to make everything okay.

And the closer I get to the hospital, the better I feel. I actually believe God is taking care of everything. So I walk onto my mom's floor, and I'm feeling pretty relaxed. Then I see my dad coming out of Mom's room.

I know immediately that all is not well. His face looks gray and worn and weary, like he's aged at least ten years in the last twenty-four hours.

"What's wrong?" I ask as he leads me over to a corner where several chairs are arranged around a coffee table.

"Sit down."

"What's wrong?" I ask again as I sit.

"It's serious, Kim." His voice breaks, and he leans forward and puts his head into his hands and just starts to sob.

Okay, now this totally unglues me. I mean, I consider myself a pretty stable, not highly emotional person, but seeing my dad falling apart is killing me. My heart is racing, and my hands are shaking, and it's like my whole world is caving in right now. I feel like I can't even breathe.

"What's wrong?" I ask again, but my voice sounds small and far off, as if it's coming from someone else.

Finally, my dad looks up at me with red, watery eyes. "Your mom has ovarian cancer."

"And that's serious?" I ask stupidly. Of course, it's serious.

He nods.

"But aren't there lots of cures and treatments for cancer?"

He nods again, but his expression is not hopeful.

"So she'll have these treatments and everything will be—"

"This is stage four ovarian cancer, Kim." The way he says stage four sounds very serious.

"Stage four?"

"Very advanced."

"What does that mean?"

He takes in a deep breath, and I can tell this is extremely painful and difficult for him. "It means the cancer has spread. It's in vital organs…"

"And that means?"

"The doctor gives her six months to a year."

I just shake my head in total disbelief. But hot tears are streaming down my face now. "It can't be! Dad, this cannot be true!"

Then he takes me in his arms, and we hold on to each other like I used to do when I was a little girl, and we both just cry. For a long time.

Everything in me is hurting now. I honestly don't know when I've ever felt so bad. So hopeless. So frightened. Finally we let go and just sit there looking at each other.

"What about a second opinion?" I say suddenly. "Aren't you supposed to get a—?"

"This is a hospital, Kim. Lots of doctors have been looking at her. Lots of tests have been done."

"How—how's Mom doing?"

"She doesn't know yet."

I feel like someone has just pulled the plug on me, like all the life is being sucked out right now, and I'm deflated and empty and useless. "Who's going to tell her?"

"I am."

"Oh, Dad." Then I reach over and hug him again. "This is so horrible. So unfair. It can't really be happening, can it?"

"I'd give anything to change it, Kim. Anything."

We sit there in silence for several minutes. I honestly can't think of a thing to say. It's as if I'm frozen in time, like life is standing still, and yet I know that it's not. If what the doctors say is true, my mom's life is spinning away—much too fast. And there's nothing—not one thing—I can do to stop it.

Finally, my dad excuses himself to go in and talk to Mom. And although I'm feeling a little irked at God right now—like why didn't He stop this?—I still pray. I pray that God will help my dad right now, help him to say the right things to my mom.

But I also pray that God will change this whole recent chain of events. Maybe the doctors made a mistake, or maybe God wants to do some kind of miraculous healing—whatever it takes, I'm praying that He will come through for us.

It's around four o'clock when my dad comes out of Mom's room, and he looks worse than ever. "She wants to see you," is all he says.

"But what do I say?"

"I don't know, Kim." He shakes his head. "I'm going to the chapel."

So I go into my mom's room. I'm expecting the worst—more emotions, more tears, more unanswerable questions—but I am surprised to see she's smiling. "Come here, sweetheart." She reaches for my hand. When I get closer to her, I can see she's been crying.

"Oh, Mom." I give her my hand and then lean down and place my head against her shoulder. "Why is this happening?"

She strokes my hair. "I don't know why, Kimmy. I don't know why."

We stay like that for a while, and finally I stand up, but I don't let go of her hand. "I didn't think you were this sick, Mom. I thought it was just the change, that you were going to be fine—" My voice breaks now. "I've been praying and believing that everything was going to be fine—and it's—"

"Everything is going to be fine, Kim. Just wait and see."

"But what about—?"

"Like I told your dad, sweetheart, this is all in God's hands. There's nothing to fear."

"You're not afraid?"

She considers this. "Well, I can't say I'm not afraid. But I trust God. I know that I'm in His hands. I know that He's watching over me. I have this deep sense of peace inside."

"Really and truly?" I study her closely. I mean, I've known this woman for almost my entire life, and she's really a bad liar. I can usually tell if she's keeping something from me.

"Really and truly."

"So what does that mean? That deep peace? Do you think you're going to get well after all?"

"I'm not sure. Maybe that's it. I can't even explain it, Kim. But it came over me last night. I was wide awake and just thinking and praying, and suddenly I got this deep sense of peace, and I knew it was from God, and I knew that everything was going to be all right."

I feel a surge of hope now. "You're certain that it's going to be all right?"

She nods. "I'm certain."

Suddenly it feels like I can breathe again. Okay, I'm not completely relieved, and I can't say that I'm not afraid. But I do have this sliver of hope running through me now. And my mom's not the kind of person to mislead anyone. She is the most honest person I know.

"I've been praying for you," I say. "A lot."

"I know. I can tell."

And then I tell her that other people are praying for her. And I promise to have all my friends praying for her. And before long, I'm beginning to believe that perhaps this is what God wants. He wants it to look like my mom is seriously ill, but then He wants to do a miracle. And what better person to do a miracle for than my mom?

"I think you're right," I finally tell her. "I think it's going to be okay."

She smiles, and I am absolutely certain that my mom has the sweetest smile on the planet. "Yes, I think you're right."

Now my dad is back, standing like a shadow in the doorway.

"Come in, Allen," my mom calls to him. Then she takes both our hands and smiles. "My two favorite people."

My dad looks amazingly recovered, or else he's putting on a brave front for my mom. "How are you doing, honey?"

"I feel better."

Now Dad turns to me. "We need to discuss some things, Kim. Medical things about treatment and whatnot. Do you want to hang around, or do you have things you need to do?"

I look at my mom. "What do you want me to do, Mom?"

"I want you to keep doing what you normally do, sweetheart. Keep your grades up and keep practicing violin and writing the column." She chuckles now. "A nurse was talking about that column today."

"Really?"

"She knew your dad was the editor, and she wanted to know who Jamie is."

"Did you tell her?" I ask.

"Of course not. But she told me that her fourteen-year-old daughter reads "Just Ask" religiously, and it seems to be the only source of advice she'll actually listen to. The nurse said she wanted to send Jamie a box of chocolates."

I kind of laugh. "Tell her just to send it care of the paper."

My dad smiles as he shakes his finger at me. "No bribes or gifts for columnists."

I turn back to my mom now. "Okay, I guess I should go. Our Christmas concert is less than two weeks away, and I've got a solo I should be practicing. Not to mention homework and those never-ending letters."

My mom is beaming up at me. "I'm so proud of you, Kimmy."

"Take it easy," I tell her. And as I'm leaving the hospital, I realize that I didn't even ask her if she was coming home today. Somehow I don't think so.

As I drive toward home, I'm feeling this crazy mix of emotions. I mean, on one hand I feel like my heart's been torn from my chest and thrown into a food processor. But on the other hand, I have this unexplainable hope too. I remember how my mom looked so certain when she assured me that everything's going to be fine. How can I not believe her?

Even so, I call Natalie as soon as I get home. I pour out the whole story, and she is very sympathetic. When I get to the part about my mom's peace and how I'm thinking it might be a God-thing, she becomes very excited.

"I can really see that," she says with enthusiasm. "God could be so glorified in this, Kim. I mean, everyone loves your mom, and I'm sure everyone will be praying for her. And when she beats this thing, it'll be so miraculous that everyone will be praising God. It'll be totally amazing!"

"Yeah, that's kind of what I'm thinking."

"I'm going to call our church prayer chain first thing," she says as we finish our conversation. "We have like five hundred people on it, and they are all seriously into prayer."

I thank her and hang up. Then, like I promised my mom, I go through the paces of practicing violin and homework. But to be honest, it feels like just motions, as if something inside of me is dead or dying. I tell myself that I'm just imagining it, that everything is going to be okay, but it's not working. Finally, in my last attempt to distract myself, I pick up the package of new "Just Ask" letters and absently peruse through several before a certain one totally stops me in my tracks.

Dear Jamie,

Why do bad things happen to good people? My grandma is the kindest person I know. She helps her neighbors and takes in stray cats and gives money to charity and knits baby blankets for orphans in Romania and all kinds of stuff. I mean, she's almost like a saint. And then just last week, she was on her way to the grocery store and got hit by a car. Now she's in a coma and critical condition and may not recover at all. So, what's up with that? Why is God so freaking mean anyway?

Confused and Angry

Okay, this is a tough one. I mean, I know how this kid feels, and I kind of feel the same way. And yet I'm supposed to write something honest and hopeful and encouraging. Finally, I know that all I can do is to ask God for help. So I actually kneel down (an action I usually reserve for only the most serious of prayers), and I beg God to bring some sense out of what feels like senseless and random acts of brutality. Like why did this sweet grandmother get struck down like that? I'd like to know myself. And why did my mom get diagnosed with stage four ovarian cancer today?

I pray and pray—and I am brutally honest with God; Chloe Miller was the one who always told me that He can take it. I tell God that, like that letter writer, I'm confused and angry too. I tell Him that life doesn't make sense sometimes. And that, although I want to believe He's got a bigger plan and can bring good out of this, like my mom and Natalie are believing—and like I want to believe too—sometimes it just seems too hard to go on.

And finally, I feel an answer coming. Oh, it's probably not a complete answer, and it might not even be the perfect answer, but I do get the impression it's coming from God, and all I can do is sit down and write it.

Dear Confused and Angry,

I know how you feel. Sometimes life makes no sense to me either. Like when someone who's bad gets away with murder, and then someone who's good gets a terminal illness. It just seems all wrong. But then I have to remind myself that I'm only seeing one tiny part of an enormous picture. It's like you're watching this epic movie being filmed, but all you see is a fraction of one scene, and the editing and sound haven't even been added. As a result, it doesn't make sense.

I think life can be like that. It's as if we're all just a small part of this bigger picture, but all we can see is what's going on around us—and sometimes it seems crazy and futile and needlessly painful. But that's why

we need God in our lives. Because I believe He's the
creator of the whole complete picture, and He has ways
of working it out so it all makes sense in the end. In the
meantime, we have to trust Him. We have to believe
that, like a director of a movie, He knows what goes
where and when and why. And if we play our parts, it
will all work out in time. I believe our role is to have
faith as we follow His direction and then to trust Him
and hope for the best. That's what I'm trying to do. I
hope this helps some. And I'm sorry about your
grandma.

    Just Jamie

Somehow I feel better after writing that. I'm not totally sure why since it doesn't really change anything. Okay, maybe it changes me. Maybe that's what God is up to right now—<u>changing me</u>. Or maybe that's the only part of this big-picture thing that I actually have any control over. Meaning I can control my own choices—like whether I choose to walk in faith or I choose to walk in fear. I'd rather walk in faith. I think that's what my mom's doing right now. And I guess if she can do it, I can at least give it my best shot.

And sure, I don't know what's around the next corner. Does anyone? But I can hang on to God and trust that He knows. And when I'm feeling lost or confused or angry (as I expect I will from time to time), I can take these things to Him and ask for help. I think that's what He wants us to do. To just ask.

Reader's Guide

1. What were your first impressions of Kim? After you read more of the story, were you right or wrong about anything? Explain.

2. Why do you think Kim's dad had such confidence that Kim could pull off a teen advice column? Did you think she could do it? Could you do it?

3. Why do you think Kim was so impacted by Tiffany Knight's death?

4. Because of her Korean heritage, Kim had been interested in Buddhism. What caused her to eventually become disenchanted with it?

5. Were you surprised at Kim's reaction to seeing the *Passion of the Christ* movie? Have you seen that film? If so, how did it impact you?

6. Kim and Cesar seem to have a good relationship. Do you think they should consider dating each other at some point in time? Why or why not?

7. Natalie is really opposed to Kim dating a non-Christian. What is your opinion on this?

8. Alcohol becomes an issue before the Harvest Dance. How do you think things could've been handled differently? What would you do under the same circumstances?

9. Were you surprised to find out that Kim's mother has such a serious illness? What would you say to Kim if you were her friend?

10. Natalie and Kim (and many others) commit themselves to pray for Mrs. Peterson's healing. Do you believe that God can heal? Do you think He'll heal Kim's mom? Why or why not?

experience

MelodyCarlson

real life. **right now.**

Diary of a Teenage Girl Series

Chloe

Diaries Are a Girl's Best Friend

MY NAME IS CHLOE, Chloe book one

Chloe Miller, Josh's younger sister, is a free spirit with dramatic clothes and hair. She struggles with her identity, classmates, parents, boys, and whether or not God is for real. But this unconventional high school freshman definitely doesn't hold back when she meets Him in a big, personal way. Chloe expresses God's love and grace through the girl band, Redemption, that she forms, and continues to show the world she's not willing to conform to anyone else's image of who or what she should be. Except God's, that is.
ISBN 1-59052-018-1

SOLD OUT, Chloe book two

Chloe and her fellow band members must sort out their lives as they become a hit in the local community. And after a talent scout from Nashville discovers the trio, all too soon their explosive musical ministry begins to encounter conflicts with family, so-called friends, and school. Exhilarated yet frustrated, Chloe puts her dream in God's hand and prays for Him to work out the details.
ISBN 1-59052-141-2

ROAD TRIP, Chloe book three

After signing with a major record company, Redemption's dreams are coming true. Chloe, Allie, and Laura begin their concert tour with the good-looking guys in the band Iron Cross. But as soon as the glitz and glamour wear off, the girls find life on the road a little overwhelming. Even rock-solid Laura appears to be feeling the stress—and Chloe isn't quite sure how to confront her about the growing signs of drug addiction...
ISBN 1-59052-142-0

FACE THE MUSIC, Chloe book four

Redemption has made it to the bestseller chart, but what Chloe and the girls need most is some downtime to sift through the usual high school stress with grades, friends, guys, and the prom. Chloe struggles to recover from a serious crush on the band leader of Iron Cross. Then just as an unexpected romance catches Redemption by surprise, Caitlin O'Conner—whose relationship with Josh is taking on a new dimension—joins the tour as a chaperone. Chloe's wild ride only speeds up, and this one-of-a-kind musician faces the fact that life may never be normal again.
ISBN 1-59052-241-9

Log on to www.DOATG.com

ALSO FROM MELODY CARLSON

Dark Blue: *Color Me Lonely*
Brutally ditched by her best friend, Kara feels totally abandoned until she discovers these dark blue days contain a life-changing secret. 1-57683-529-4

Deep Green: *Color Me Jealous*
Stuck in a twisted love triangle, Jordan feels absolutely green with envy until her former best friend, Kara, introduces her to someone even more important than Timothy. 1-57683-530-8

Torch Red: *Color Me Torn*
Zoë feels like the only virgin on Earth. But now that she's dating Justin Clark, that seems like it's about to change. Luckily, Zoë's friend Nate is there to try to save her from the biggest mistake of her life.
1-57683-531-6

Pitch Black: *Color Me Lost*
Following her friend's suicide, Morgan questions the meaning of life and death and God. As she struggles with her grief, Morgan must make her life's ultimate decision—before it's too late. 1-57683-532-4

Burnt Orange: *Color Me Wasted*
Amber Conrad has a problem. Her youth group friends Simi and Lisa won't get off her case about the drinking parties she's been going to. *Everyone does it. What's the big deal?* Will she be honest with herself and her friends before things really get out of control? 1-57683-533-2

Look for the TrueColors series at a Christian bookstore near you or order online at www.navpress.com.

truecolors

THINK